Bob Kelly has been practicing criminal defense and family court litigation for the past 28 years in Upstate New York. He grew up in Chicago and has a passion for the city and its people. He has a degree in English literature from the University of Wisconsin and a JD from Chicago-Kent College of Law.

This book is dedicated to my mom, Jane Suttle, who inspired me with optimism, imagination and love.

Bob Kelly

CHICAGO DETECTIVE JACK FALLON IN THE MYSTERY OF THE EXOTIC ESCORT MURDERS

AUSTIN MACAULEY PUBLISHERS™

LONDON ∗ CAMBRIDGE ∗ NEW YORK ∗ SHARJAH

Ordering Information
Quantity sales: Special discounts are available on quantity purchases by corporations, associations, and others. For details, contact the publisher at the address below.

Publisher's Cataloging-in-Publication data
Kelly, Bob
Chicago Detective Jack Fallon in the Mystery of the Exotic Escort Murders

ISBN 9781638296904 (Paperback)
ISBN 9781638296911 (Hardback)
ISBN 9781638296935 (ePub e-book)
ISBN 9781638296928 (Audiobook)

Library of Congress Control Number: 2022918795

www.austinmacauley.com/us

First Published 2022
Austin Macauley Publishers LLC
40 Wall Street, 33rd Floor, Suite 3302
New York, NY 10005
USA

mail-usa@austinmacauley.com
+1 (646) 5125767

20230119

My thanks to Mike Valentino for rough editing and to Morgan Beldock and Jason Smith for technical support.

Chapter 1

I found myself walking along inner-Lakeshore Drive between Chicago Avenue and Ohio Street. The sun was shining on a cold day in early April, it was 38 degrees but felt much colder with the gusty breeze we call the hawk whipping in from the Lake. I was thinking it's good that the Cubs are out of town. The White Sox were on their own that day. The only thing I was worried about from the South Side was the possibility of some young muggers that had been blitzing pedestrians in the Streeterville neighborhood by jumping out of cars and taking cell phones, purses, backpacks, and computer cases. They had been attacking men and women, young and old, day and night, and then hopping back in their cars and driving out of the neighborhood. The theory was that they were then getting on Lakeshore Drive and heading south.

It was around 10 a.m. and I was getting cold. The Lake was rough that day with the wind pushing three-foot waves crashing onto the shore. I was doing a good job looking like a tourist just daydreaming and talking on what looked like an expensive smart phone. I was in fact talking on my own smart phone but not the one in my right hand. I had an ear bud and mic so that my new partner Elaina Rodriguez, who was shadowing me in an unmarked car trying not to be obvious, could hear me. My phone was in my inner jacket pocket along with my detective's star. While I am normally a pretty confident 29-year-old Chicago detective, I was feeling distinctly like a sitting duck that was trying hard to be aware of his surroundings while looking like a clueless tourist at the same time. Every car that went by could be the one. Every approaching young man was a suspect, even though in theory I was looking for only young black men.

I saw Rodriguez coming up behind me as I crossed Superior Street near Northwestern University's Abbott Hall. I didn't look at her as she drove past and turned right onto Huron Street. I suggested that she might enjoy a nice walk in the fresh air, and she reminded me that even though she was new to

Area Three at the Near North, she was still the senior partner. I just chuckled and told her that when I went a couple more blocks and got to the W Lakeshore Hotel, I was going to turn right onto Ontario Street and walk a few blocks toward Michigan Avenue. She said okay and kept going.

There wasn't much small talk with Elaina, I didn't really know her very well. My first partner was a detective named Vernon Johnson. For the past 2 1/2 years he was great to work with. He was 40 years old and had seen it all. There was never a situation that came up that he hadn't handled, so I was surprised and disappointed when he put in for a transfer to go back to District 15 in Area Five. I had done my patrolman time in that Area and had grown up near Austin in the Gale Wood neighborhood. Austin is a rough place even by Chicago standards, and I couldn't wait to get out of there. I made detective and felt lucky to get assigned to District 18 in the Near North which includes Streeterville and River North. Michigan Avenue's "Magnificent Mile" runs right through the heart of my District; it is a bustling, vibrant place with a lot of expensive hotels, condos, and apartments. Of course, it also has its share of homeless and the daily influx of service workers and students that flood the Near North from other neighborhoods in the city and suburbs. The area is also full of visiting tourists and businesspeople, so basically there is no way to really tell who belongs, but I was trying to keep an eye out for approaching young black men on foot or in cars. I've already gone on alert for more than a dozen false alarms. As I walked past the W Lakeshore. I looked over to see the waves pounding the lake path and Ohio Street Beach. Just beyond the beach I could see the Ferris wheel at Navy Pier and allowed myself to think about how great Chicago summers are as I pulled my navy-blue Bears knit hat tighter down over my head.

Rodriguez drove by again. I didn't look at her as I turned to walk up Ontario. I couldn't help thinking that it was now going to get darker and colder as I walked, and I quickly lost the sun and the wind seemed to become stronger and more focused with the tall buildings creating a long cold wind tunnel. I saw some people walking ahead of me going in the same direction on the other side of the street and then on my side of Ontario on the sidewalk an older white guy, obviously homeless, was sitting on some flattened cardboard holding a paper cup containing some coins that he was jingling and hoping for more. I couldn't tell whether he was purposely shaking the cup or was merely shivering due to the cold biting wind. Just as I was deciding whether I should play the tourist and drop the guy some change I heard the screech of tires on pavement. I had let my guard down. Where the hell was Rodriguez! In a flash the first guy coming out of the passenger side front seat was on me. He's a young black man about my height of six two but more slender, about 170 pounds. The guy ran right into my straight right hand which was holding the decoy cell phone. I hit him hard in his left eye and he howled in pain as the edge of the cell phone penetrated his eye and blood gushes out. Immediately the second guy came bolting out of the backseat. I flicked out a quick left jab, but it just pushed him back for a second. He was about 5'10" and well-built at approximately 190 pounds. I couldn't see the third man who had gotten out of the driver's seat and come around the front of their gold Honda Accord. He hit me from behind with a hard tackle that put me on the sidewalk face first. I barely got my hands out in front of me before everything came crashing down. I lost the phone as my hands and chin scraped their way forward on the cement. The mugger started pummeling the back of my head while also trying to go through my pants pockets and my jacket. He was trying to unzip the coat pocket holding my cell phone but I was struggling to knock him off me. I could tell that he was big and strong, and he started yelling to the second guy, "Kick him in the head, kick the motherfucker in the head!"

Out of the corner of my left eye I saw something dark; I turned my head away from it and tried to roll over as a kick hit my left shoulder. The second kick glanced off the top of my head knocking my hat off and sending it a couple of feet away. I was thinking if one of these guys finds the gun strapped to my ankle on my right leg I'm screwed.

There were more screeching tires and the sound of a car door slamming shut and then a body was flying over me from the street. Suddenly, the weight was off me and I saw Rodriguez and the third attacker rolling across the sidewalk right into the old homeless guy who was still sitting in the same place looking bewildered and then getting tangled up with these two rolling around on his cardboard. I jumped up and saw the stocky kid dragging the slender guy who was still bleeding from his eye and whimpering into the car. I reached their car in just a few strides but they were too quick. They got the doors locked and I heard the engine roar to life. Meanwhile, Elaina had left our vehicle running. I got to it in a flash. I was on the chase.

I called out to Rodriguez, "Are you all right?"

I turned to see her pounding the guy's head face first into the cardboard and reaching for her cuffs. "I got this," she said, "go, just go, okay!"

They had about a half block lead on me and they weren't driving carefully. The traffic on that Tuesday morning was relatively light, but heading toward Michigan Avenue it picked up. I grabbed the blue light from the floor, put it on the dashboard, and hit the siren and the accelerator. Vehicles pulled over to the left but a guy in a black Mazda froze and I narrowly miss him. Up ahead I could see the gold Honda had busted through a red light at McClurg Court and I had to do the same, bobbing and weaving to keep up to the next cross street which was Fairbanks. They could go either way to get on Lakeshore Drive at Chicago Avenue to the north or go south toward one of the Lakeshore Drive entrances. I was gaining on them and they were only a couple of cars ahead of me in the right lane. I was thinking they're headed to Chicago Avenue but at the last second, they cut across the traffic and turned left just avoiding a white delivery truck and a couple of young women in the intersection. I swerved left and narrowly missed the same delivery truck which stopped in the middle of the road. The women made it across the street and I could see the Honda about 30 yards ahead of me.

I noticed that the steering wheel felt slippery, which I knew wasn't good. I was spurting blood from my chin; I had scraped it on the uneven part of the sidewalk. I wiped my chin on the steering wheel with the sleeve of my jacket, Damn I have no time for this. I was driving way too fast And I couldn't afford to get distracted. I was right on them and we were speeding through intersections and red lights. We crossed Ohio Street, Grand Avenue and then East Illinois Street.

I was narrating the chase on my radio, hoping that dispatch could get some patrol cars to get ahead of me somewhere to block the Honda before it could get to Randolph Street where they could cut over to Lakeshore Drive. They were going almost 80 as we headed to the double deck bridge over the Chicago River which was thrashing and rolling from the wind and waves off the lake.

They stayed on the lower level which becomes a tunnel for a few blocks that is its own little world of homeless people who have staked out a few feet of sidewalk. The wail of the siren was really amplified in the tunnel and the blue pulsing light bounced off the tunnel surfaces making the entire atmosphere seem surreal. We charged out of the darkness into bright sunlight on Columbus Drive. Luckily, the traffic there wasn't too bad but at 80 miles an

12

hour I was worried that someone, including me, could get killed. At South Water Street I could see a blue Chevy starting to come off a stop sign beginning to turn right into the path of the Honda.

A terrible collision seemed inevitable. The older woman driving the Chevy must have been oblivious to the situation and just kept coming. The young stocky kid driving the Honda showed amazingly quick reflexes pulling around the Chevy into the oncoming lane which had a Dodge pickup in it. The guy driving it couldn't find a place on the right to pull over. With catlike quickness the Honda driver avoided the pickup, careened back into his driving lane and accelerated. This maneuver caused me to fall behind them a little but I punched the gas. Just then I heard dispatch say that they have set up a roadblock on Columbus Drive just before Randolph Street. They had gotten permission from command and at that moment a marked car pulled out ahead of me to take the lead in the pursuit. Protocol tells me to back off from the chase, but my adrenaline was raging so much my back off was minimal. The only thing that I had been able to determine about what was going on in the gold Honda was that the stocky guy was driving and wearing a green sweatshirt. The guy I popped in the eye was slumped forward in the passenger seat.

The last couple of small side streets had been blocked off with a barricade of patrol cars, leaving no escape routes before we all ran into what was waiting at Randolph Street.

They had gotten organized incredibly quickly. There were cars and wagons lined up across the north side of Randolph, blocking entry into the Millennium Park area. It was critical to keep them out of there because it being Easter week, the town was full of tourists on spring break, including many groups of high school and college kids as well as groups from Japan, Germany and God knows where else.

The lead chase car was right on the Honda, siren blasting in concert with mine.

All the cars and lights flashing created quite a scene, attracting onlookers on the sidewalks and a gathering crowd from across Randolph Street. at the edge of Millennium Park, I was thinking that this is happening too fast for anything good to come out of it. The Honda was now only 50 yards away from the blockade and the patrol car started to slow down and move left. I continued to follow directly behind the Honda, but I needed to hit the brakes as I approached the blockade. I could see that the stocky driver was cutting it way too close. At the last possible second, he made a hard turn right with tires screeching and burning. The car fishtailed almost into the blockade of cars and officers with their guns drawn.

He was going for a small sliver of daylight between the last car and a streetlight on the corner next to a fire hydrant. There seemed to be no way to get through. The Honda slammed into the streetlight and bounces off it into the fire hydrant. It opened up like a geyser and the car came to a halt. Everything was in slow motion.

I was now close enough to see the impact. The airbags exploded outward into the driver and the passenger who were not wearing seatbelts. Both doors flew open and I could see the passenger fall limply out and just land partially out of the car with the water from the fire hydrant cascading over him. Amazingly, the driver leapt out of the car like a cat and ran right past a couple of officers and a few gawkers. He bounded across Randolph and I didn't think, I just ran after him. I didn't know whether anybody else was joining the chase. I couldn't think of anything else except nailing him. He ran through the onlookers on the sidewalk, across the street and into Millennium Park toward the Pritzker Pavilion. At this point the foot traffic was light and there wasn't anything going on at the Pavilion.

Unfortunately, the stocky kid ran as fast as I did and the adrenaline was wearing off and I was starting to feel pain, not only from my still bleeding chin but from the side of my left temple where I got kicked. A lump the size of an egg that had developed on my left temple and was throbbing. I also noticed that my pant legs were ripped and I had a nice raspberry scrape on my left knee which didn't feel so hot either but I was in pretty good shape and highly motivated to catch the bastard. I kept running. He was about 25 yards ahead of me and in view. He was wearing a green sweatshirt with something on the front, but I couldn't really make it out. He was also wearing blue jeans with dark sneakers.

He ran through the pavilion area, dodging in and around small groups of tourists and headed toward the center of the park toward Cloud Gate. He came upon a large group of high school kids and ran right through them. He had no problem pushing through the crowd and knocked two girls to the ground. One kid started screaming and it was so chaotic that I had to slow down and weave my way through a couple of dozen startled teenagers to untangle myself from this group.

He had opened up some distance from me. I could see that he was heading toward where there were several other groups milling around the Bean taking pictures and gazing into their reflections. He ran into a guy who had stepped in front of him to take a picture of his companion and that gave me a little chance for catching up. He didn't hesitate to run right under the Bean and I lost sight of him.

When I get through to the other side of Cloud Gate, I was not sure which way he had gone. I had to step back to look for him. I looked left and didn't see him but on the right, I glimpsed the top of his head and a sliver of his green sweatshirt.

I could see that he was running through another group of high school kids toward Wrigley Square in the northwest corner of the park. By the time I reached that high school group he was gone again. I looked all around but he was nowhere in sight. There was a large group of young college students gathered around the monument of Doric style columns. I ran up to the monument and jumped up on it and tried to spot my guy but he was gone. For the first time I noticed that a couple of uniform officers had been trailing me. I told one of them to call it in and that the suspect had exited the park at Michigan and Randolph. He could be headed for Millennium Station for a commuter train south or several subway or L stations as well as buses going south on Michigan Avenue. I also told them that I would check in with the station after I got out of the hospital. Sweat and blood were drying on my face from the cold Chicago wind. Suddenly I felt extremely exhausted but so extremely alive.

Chapter 2

I walked out of Northwestern Memorial Hospital two hours after walking in with eight stitches on my chin, a bandage on my scraped up left knee, and a throbbing headache. I had an ice pack for the bump on my head, my left eye looked like it had met a right hook from Mike Tyson and I figured when you feel good you look good.

The patrol car that I had called for was sitting on Erie Street waiting for me. I got into the passenger side and nodded to a patrolman that I had never seen before. He was clearly trying very hard not to look at me. Apparently, I looked as bad as I felt. He didn't say a word during the short ride to Area Three Headquarters. It seemed unusually quiet inside the station. Irene, the desk sergeant, waved me over to her and chuckled. "You look like hell Fallon. Better get into the briefing room. They found another dead woman, this time at the Ritz Carlton. Captain Corcoran is in there having a fit."

I opened the door and moved forward as stealthily as possible, gently trying to be invisible as I tiptoed in. The Captain scowled at me and said, "Sit the hell down, Fallon." I took the first seat available and sat down feeling surprised on two counts. First, we rarely have any direct contact with Captains, they are more administration than field officers and report directly to the Area Command. Secondly, I certainly did not think that he knew who I was. I guess I hadn't missed much because he said, "I'm going to lay this all out for you from the beginning." I was glad to hear that since I had no idea what he was talking about. The room was full of mostly detectives and a few high-ranking patrol officers. I noticed that Rodriguez was sitting up front and I remember thinking that it would be nice to see her report before I wrote mine. Some things were still a little fuzzy in my mind.

Corcoran cleared his throat and walked over to a large street map of the Streeterville and the River North neighborhoods. He placed red colored pushpins at three spots on the map and cleared his throat again. "This morning a third young woman's body was found at one of the area's high-end hotels. This one was found in a room on the 20th floor of the Ritz-Carlton at Water Tower Place. She had an ice pick stuck in her eye. As far as I know they don't serve ice picks with their champagne at the Ritz. This makes three young women in three weeks in the Near the North.

"The first one was found at the Peninsula Hotel on East Superior Street two weeks ago. The second woman was found strangled in a room at the London House on East Wacker last week. We're still not sure about the cause of death of the first victim. None of the women were found with cell phones or identification. All three were in their mid-20s, attractive and found naked in bed. So far, we have a white girl, a black girl and this last one is Asian. Commander Hawkins wants this given top priority.

"I'm going to form a task force of five detective teams full-time on this case. This task force will be given priority and CSI and patrol resources as needed."

I looked around the room and I couldn't help but feel excited. I had been trying to get assigned to Homicide for about a year, but it wasn't easy because my partner Vernon Johnson had been on the force for 18 years and didn't really push for the change. All Vernon really wanted was to get transferred back to the Austin area. This was my first day on the job with my new partner Elaina Rodriguez and I had no idea how she felt about going to Homicide. I only knew that she was 33, came on the force after three years in the Army, was athletic and not afraid to mix it up. She was also attractive and wears a wedding ring.

Captain Corcoran was getting ready to wrap it up. "I am assigning three pairs of detectives that have already been working primarily homicide investigations and two pair that have been dealing with robbery and vice." He then began calling out the pairs, first the homicide veterans. He started with Detective Sgt. Clyde Simpson and his partner Detective James "Jimmy" Stone. Simpson grew up in North Lawndale on the West Side and went to Manley High School before getting a four-year degree in criminal justice from Chicago State University. Jimmy Stone had partnered with Clyde Simpson for about three years. He is from Beverly on the far Southwest side of the city, and went to Mount Carmel High School. He played football against Fenwick where I went when he was a senior and I was a sophomore. Mount Caramel won that one and he likes to remind me of that often. He is a lot like Simpson, and they seem to get along well.

Next the Captain called out Detective Zileen Baker, age 39. She is from Woodlawn on the South Side and attended Hyde Park Academy. She got a full academic scholarship to the University of Illinois at Champaign and is probably the smartest detective I have met so far. Ironically, she is paired with Frank Kozlowski better known as Koz who was probably the biggest jerk that I have run across so far. Frank grew up in Avondale and went to Lane Tech, his claim to fame. I have to wonder how he passed the entrance exam to get in there. He enlisted in the Navy for two years then did a year at community college before starting with the CPD. He is 41 and about a year and a half from his 20-year retirement. I for one am looking forward to it more than he is. I don't know how Zileen stands it.

The last pair of homicide detectives are Morgan Latner, age 32 and Henrique Sanchez, 34. Latner is from Evanston and went to high school there. He played basketball at Evanston and was pretty damn good. He was one of the biggest guys on the detective squad basketball team that I play on and, not surprisingly, one of our best players. Now living in the North Side's Edgewater neighborhood, he got a degree in law enforcement and criminal justice at Oakton Community College. Latner is partnered with Henrique Sanchez, who is from Humboldt Park in the near West Side. He went to Westinghouse High School and has a degree in political science with a minor in criminology from the University of Illinois Circle Campus in Chicago. He wants to be Mayor and lets everybody know it. He is a really nice guy. Everybody except Kos likes him.

Corcoran cleared his throat one more time and called out Detective Richard Ricky Del Signore He is one of the few detectives that I knew who was younger than me. He was from the North Side, West Rogers Park area and attended McArthur High School. He was good enough at baseball to get a scholarship to Illinois State. At 27 he was a good athlete and also played on our basketball team. He lived near Loyola University in Rogers Park. He was partnered with Detective Carl Schmidt, age 38. He grew up in Lincoln Square in the middle of the North Side and went to Schurz High School. He was a big burly guy who had played football at Schurz. He still lived in Lincoln Square and was married with four kids. Ricky liked Schmidt and said that he had helped him greatly and had his back in some pretty tough situations. The Captain said he was welcoming Elaina Rodriguez to the Near North with this assignment. He noted that she had already had an eventful morning on her first day. Everybody looked at Elaina and said hi there, and waved and nodded in her direction, except of course Koz. "Looks like Fallon had a more eventful day than she did," he said, "and she had to save his ass."

Captain Corcoran turned bright red. "Knock it off, Kozlowski. If you don't want this assignment, tell me now…otherwise shut the fuck up." Koz had a big grin on his face but decided to shut the fuck up after the Captain finished staring a hole in him.

Corcoran then said, "Okay. You ten will report to Lieutenant Whitehead in his office right now. I want progress reports every day. Get going."

We all filed out of the briefing room and walked up the stairs to Lieutenant Tyrone Whitehead's office. Whitehead was a very large, imposing black man, standing 6'6" and obviously in good shape. The door to his spacious office was open and he waved us in from behind a big desk that somehow didn't seem quite large enough for the Lieutenant There were six chairs. Elaina and I along with Del Signore and Latner ended up standing along the wall. Rodriguez looked at me and whispered, "You look terrible."

I muttered, "Thanks for getting that guy off me."

Whitehead told us to knock it off. Everybody turned their attention to him. "As you people know, we are getting a lot of pressure already from the mayor's office. She's pressing Command and that gets put on us. Three dead young women within three weeks at four- and five-star hotels in the Near North is sending a shock to these businesses. The last thing they need is something that could scare people away after they are finally getting back on firm ground after the virus.

"I want to split this up like this. I want thorough victimology on the three women. Baker, you and Koz take the first victim. Get in touch with the medical examiner's office and pin down the cause of death as soon as possible. We are releasing pictures of the women from security cameras in the three hotels. No information about the cause of death is being made public. We hope to have leads on the identities from the tip line. Simpson and Stone, you take the second victim from the Peninsula; she apparently was strangled but confirm this with the ME and coordinate with Crime Scene. Simpson, you are the only sergeant in this group so if something comes up you make the call. I will also want you to stay in touch with each group and brief me daily. I will report to the Captain."

Whitehead let Latner and Sanchez take victim number three. "We know she ended up with an ice pick in her eye but check with the ME after the autopsy. I want to know the toxicology on all three. You will be responsible for looking at the closed circuit from the hotel where the victims were found. Obviously look for the victims and anyone that they can be seen with. We should be able to see the perp or perps from the hallway cameras. That should keep you busy for a while."

"Del Signore, Schmidt, Rodriguez and Fallon, I want you to divide the tips that come in and canvas the high-end restaurants and hotels with the victims' pictures. Del Signore and Schmidt, take Streeterville. everything from the East Side of Michigan Avenue to the lake. Rodriguez and Fallon, take everything from the West Side of Michigan Ave. to the river in the North. Fallon, what the hell happened to you?"

"Well, I was the decoy on that mugging detail and it worked," I said. "They took the bait and it got a little rough. One got away but I think we got two of them. Haven't had a chance to check on anything."

Whitehead winced and said, "At least Rodriguez got one. The other two took off. One is in the wind and the other guy died at the scene. We're not sure if he was dead before or after the crash. He broke his neck. I'm giving that case to Youngblood and Skinner. Write your report and get it on my desk by tomorrow.

"Fallon, I also want to see your discharge from Northwestern, if you have a concussion, you're out of this."

"I don't, Lieutenant. I'm just sore, I'll be fine."

"Okay, your report on the discharge tomorrow. You're all dismissed. Don't let me down."

I pulled Rodriguez aside and said, "Okay, partner, let's get a beer."

She nodded and I said, "Meet me at Timothy O'Toole's on Ontario and Fairbanks in ten minutes."

I parked near the corner on Fairbanks and looked down the road I had traveled under much different circumstances just three hours earlier. I just kind of shook my head and walked into one of my favorite Chicago establishments.

Elaina was already sitting at the bar in this classic pub filled with black barstools and wooden tables and chairs rich with light and dark brown hues and lit up by little lights and mirrors and decorations of beer signs and sports memorabilia. The lunch crowd had thinned out and for the first moment in what seemed like days, I let myself sit down next to my new partner and relax.

I looked at Charlie, the cute 25-year-old blonde bartender, and said, "Don't ask."

She smiled and bent down to get me a Miller High Life out of the cooler. She put three shot glasses down in front of us and poured them full with Jack Daniels. We clinked our shot glasses together and wolfed them down. She repeated the process and asked "How's the other guy doing, Jack?" I burst out laughing and so did Rodriguez.

"Seriously, there were three of them, one got away, one is in jail and one is dead."

She looked sort of surprised and said, "I guess two out of three ain't bad."

I introduced her to Elaina and asked if my older brother Barry was working there today. She said no, that he was working tonight. I explained that Barry was one of the managers at O'Toole's and that the place became like my local in the past couple of years. I took a long drink of my beer and started to feel better., I looked over to Elaina and said, "Well, welcome to the Near North." I picked up my Miller and she picked up her Corona and we clinked bottles.

"Hell of a first day," she said with a smile.

"Thanks for the help with that guy on my back, he really laid me out. He felt really strong, the only time I got a look at him, you were pounding his face into the sidewalk. I have to admit after what he did to me, I enjoyed it." She smiled again. I started to realize how attractive she is but tried not to go there.

"I was afraid to do anything else," she said, "if I let him up, I was afraid he might kill me. Luckily, the uniforms got there right after you took off chasing the other guys. What happened?" she asked.

"I chased them up Ontario until they turned left on Fairbanks. It was a pretty hairy ride. Luckily, traffic wasn't too bad but they still were going 80 on the street and stayed low on the bridge and then they got boxed in at Randolph. The driver tried to squeeze through one end of it and hit a light pole and a fire hydrant which busted the hydrant but stopped the car. The airbags popped and the passenger got tossed partly out of his side and the driver took off. I ran after him through the park but he lost me going toward Michigan and Randolph. I figure he could've headed to Millennium Station or the L on Wabash, or the subway on State or even a bus on Michigan going south.

"I guess we'll have to leave the rest to Youngblood and Skinner. I don't really like leaving this case half finished. I heard that other kid didn't survive the crash," she said.

"We're witnesses now."

"You know the guy I collared got arraigned on the attempted robbery and assault and battery," she said, "now that his partner died, he should get charged with felony murder."

"I was able to get the plate number of their car. It was stolen from Brownsville yesterday. Were you able to ID your guy?" I asked.

"Yeah, he was in the system. His name is Lucius Perkins, age 19, from Englewood. Priors aren't serious but he has a known association with the Gangster Disciples. Bail was set at $10,000 but that should go up if they can get him arraigned on the felony murder charge."

Charlie came by with two more beers and a plastic bag filled with ice for the bump on my head and three more shots.

Rodriguez and I got to know each other a little better, then decided to call it a day. She had a couple of kids to get to from daycare and I needed to get home and lick my wounds.

We agreed to talk tomorrow and figure out how to attack the tips that were sure to start flowing in.

Our new case was going to hit the evening news that night. We got up from the bar and started to leave. Elaina pulled something out of her coat pocket. "By the way, here's your hat," she said and tossed it to me.

I grabbed it out of the air with my right hand. "Thanks partner," I said. "See you tomorrow."

Chapter 3

I woke up around 7:30 with my head still pounding and an ice bag next to my pillow. My chin hurt and the scrape on my left knee made me wince every time I bent my leg.

On the other hand, the sun was shining and my ice bag now full of cold water wasn't leaking. I picked up my phone from the nightstand and sat on the edge of my king bed. I saw that Rodriguez has already sent me a couple of messages. The tips had started pouring in overnight from the evening news broadcast and Whitehead wanted us on it pronto. I shot a text to my partner saying I would be at the district headquarters at 8:30. She asked how I was feeling.

I said, "Not great but the swelling is down a bit; my black eye has also started to heal, it's now more purple and black."

I stood up, rubbed my knee and walked into the living room of my one-bedroom apartment at the Covington Apartments on N. Clarendon Ave. in Uptown. I was still getting used to the apartment and the neighborhood after moving there February 1.

My longtime girlfriend Gina Juliano and I had broken up during the Christmas season and I moved out of the apartment we'd shared in Gale Wood. After spending a month with my dad in the house I lived in for much of my childhood, I was very ready for my own space.

I looked out the bay of windows facing east past the Weiss Memorial Hospital building and parking area, and I could see the beginning of the green spaces of Lincoln Park near Wilson Beach and the skate park that leads to the famous Montrose Beach and marina, which is in an attractive part of the neighborhood. I went to the fridge which at the moment was only populated by some bottles of Miller and a carton of milk. *I've got to get to the grocery store.* I grabbed the milk and was relieved to discover that the box of Frosted Flakes on the granite counter was half full.

After my shower I put on a long sleeve blue Oxford shirt and a navy suit with a navy and green striped tie. I donned my holster and gun and put my star on my belt.

I was living on the 12th floor out of 14, so I headed to the elevator to go down to the outside covered parking area. I would have sprung for a garage if there was one available but at least the overhead cover helps. I had already dodged a couple of pretty good snowstorms since I had moved into the building.

I went to my parking space and got into my black-on-black Chevy Camaro convertible V6 335 hp and headed over to Lakeshore Drive for the short trip to my North Larrabee Street District Station. When I arrived at the station it was buzzing with activity. There were a couple of television reporters with camera crews outside on the sidewalk. One of the reporters was talking to Lieutenant Whitehead and I could hear him say something about hoping for the public's help to identify the victims.

I saw a reporter that I had recognized from one of the local TV stations spot me and started hustling toward me. I turned and hurried into the station leaving behind her questions about the victims' identities. I can only assume she was referring to the hotel murders and not the mugging case.

I walked into the large detective's room that was newly set up with desks for the 10 task force detectives with two side by side for each set of partners. I saw Rodriguez sitting at her desk and I moved into the desk next to her. Del Signore and Schmidt were at the desks closest to ours and Baker and Kozlowski were standing up front near their desks. The other four detectives were already out at their respective hotels following up on the videos. Before I could sit down.

Koz stopped talking to Baker and said loudly, "You still look like shit, Fallon."

"Thanks," I said, "I will get better in a few days and you will still be butt ugly for the rest of your life."

His face flushed with anger and he started coming toward me. I stood up and tensed for a fight. We have never liked each other but I had been able to basically avoid him most of the time. I had him by an inch at 6'2" but he had me by about 25 pounds. I wasn't afraid of him, but I knew I would have a tough fight on my hands.

His partner, Zileen Baker, calmly stepped in between us and gently put her hand on Koz' chest and said, "Koz, we need to get over to the Peninsula to start looking at their video, that's going to be enough trouble." Koz followed her out of the room but managed to bump into me on the way out. I have to admit I didn't make much of an attempt to get out of his way.

I sat down at my desk next to Rodriguez and I muttered, "What an asshole."

She looked at me and said, "He seems like such a nice guy to me."

I had to laugh too. "Okay."

"We have a ton of tips to look at," she said, "I think you should know that Lucius Perkins got bailed out before they could arraign him on the felony murder charge. Of course he's now in the wind. They identified the kid who didn't make it, his name is Michael Watkins a.k.a. Mookie. He was only 17, He died of a broken neck from the crash but he already had a lot of internal bleeding. He's also from Englewood. No luck on the third guy, but they found some closed circuit of him getting off the Green Line in Englewood. Youngblood and Skinner are going to work with the Southside gang unit to identify the stocky guy."

Elaina looked worried. "I have a bad feeling about these guys," she said, "I've seen enough witness intimidation with the Latino gangs to know that the GPs could come after us, watch your back, partner."

"Okay, I hear you," I said, "let's figure out how to divide the tips with Del Signore and Schmidt."

Since Ricky and Carl had already started, we decided they would take the leads that came in from 9:00 p.m. the time of the first evening news broadcasts until about midnight and we would take from midnight until 8:30 today. We figured the first few hours would see about the same number as the next eight.

By around 10:30 a.m. we had sifted through the calls and emails that came in from 12 to 8, most were clearly not relevant, and some were downright wacky. We were fairly confident that victim number two was not really the mayor. There were a couple that seemed promising, however. Concerning victim number three, the Asian woman found at the Ritz-Carlton, one was the Concierge at the Godfrey Hotel on West Huron, and another, a manager at one of the hot restaurants on Clark Street, The Frontera Grill.

We decided to head over to the Godfrey first, parked on Huron Street and stood outside for a moment, looking at the modern hard-edged building. It had multiple levels of rectangles of cement and glass, lots of glass.

Inside everything was slick with clean and colorful lines including reds, lots of greens and yellows. We found the front desk area. At the concierge desk, a nice-looking blonde woman named Lene, was on duty. We walked up and introduced ourselves.

She thanked us for coming and said she was the Concierge. She wanted to call because she was upset by what was happening to those poor women. She spoke perfect English but there was an accent that I couldn't place; it turned out to be Danish.

She was pretty sure that she had seen the Asian victim at the Godfrey sometime in the last week of March. She said that she was with an older gentleman and that they were having drinks at the bar. She didn't see where they went but she thought they were staying at the hotel because they didn't have coats and it was a cold March day.

We asked if she would call for a manager who we could talk to about seeing the closed circuit footage. She called someone and said he would be here in a minute.

While we waited, I noticed a group of people walking into the hotel with facemasks, not as many people were wearing them these days but you still saw them enough that they didn't seem out of place.

The Manager, George Foote, was a short slightly chubby guy in his 40s with a smiling round face. He approached us and introduced himself. We did the same. Elaina told him about the situation. I asked if they had video from the previous week and if so, could we see it.

He said he thought that would be possible and used his phone to call Security.

He said, "Okay, okay we will be right there."

We walked around the front desk and into the Security Office right behind the Command Room as he called it. It was impressive. There were eight screens that were running on real time of various floor hallways, the elevators, and in restaurant areas. In the front door area, inside and outside. There were cameras in the parking areas and backdoor areas that could be accessed by two other screens that were offered to us to go through the video of times from the last week in March. Lene suggested they had been there mid-week so I suggested that we try Tuesday or Wednesday during happy hour, 4 p.m. to 6 p.m.

After a 15-minute tutorial on the video system, we sat down in front of our screens and started with Tuesday. We got through Tuesday without seeing anything interesting. It was painstaking and frankly a bit boring but necessary. By the time we got to 5:15 on Wednesday, we had been watching for three hours. Finally we saw our girl.

She was dressed in casual chic, with form-fitting tan slacks and a light blue mildly revealing blouse and three-inch heels. She was petite, very attractive with long black hair. She was in her early to mid-20s. She was with a distinguished looking white guy around 50, dressed in a black tailored suit with a white shirt and charcoal tie.

They sat down at the bar and ordered drinks. She had some sort of a martini and he had something that looked like scotch on the rocks. They seemed to be getting along famously and were leaning into each other to talk and laugh. She was touching him in a way that a man likes to be touched when he is interested in an attractive lady. He touched her shoulder but didn't go any further. They ordered another round.

I looked at Rodriguez and asked, "What do you think?"

"I think he's either George Clooney or she's on the job."

"I'm going to go with on-the-job," I responded.

The bartender, an older guy who looked like a veteran of the downtown scene, brought them a couple more of the same and George Clooney asked for the bill. He signed the check and they got up with their drinks and walked toward the elevators.

We looked at each other and said at the same time, "We got him."

We got up and thanked the Security Manager who was sitting with us and asked him if he could get us the bar bill received from the transaction we had just watched. The previous Wednesday at 5:52 p.m., Clooney turned out to be a guy named Richard Kotler from Mequon, in Wisconsin, a nice suburb north of Milwaukee. He checked out the next day without incident. No dead bodies found in his room. He had been a frequent guest at the Godfrey over the past couple of years. There was nothing remarkable about his stays other than he often had drinks and dinner with a companion. He was the typical customer that stays at many downtown hotels for a few days for business or pleasure with a generous expense account.

Mr. Kotler used his corporate card at the Godfrey, so it didn't take us long to figure out where to find his office in downtown Milwaukee. We coordinated with the Milwaukee Police Department to go up there the next day and interview him.

It was now after three and we hadn't eaten lunch. I was starving and Rodriguez was hungry too. I suggested we get Italian beef at Al's on Wells Street near Ohio. She agreed even though she prefers Portillo's. We got to our car for the day, a blue Chevy Impala, and Rodriguez once again got in to drive. I had been learning that while she was agreeable and will often let me take the lead in situations, she'd always insist on driving. That was okay with me, especially since my previous partner Vernon Johnson, always insisted that I drive. He liked having his eyes free to watch the streets. He noticed everything and always drilled that into me to be aware of everyone and everything around me. I was thinking that if I had been a little bit more alert, I might not have had the stitches on my chin or the lump on my head.

Al's on Wells is a small classic Chicago hot dog stand type of place with about five small tables and the food being cooked and prepared behind the counter right in front of you, guys behind the counter pumping up the food, and a young woman taking orders and ringing people up. Everybody behind the counter was still wearing a mask and gloves, probably should have been doing that all along but the virus brought some permanent changes. I ordered a big beef with their signature hot jardinière fully dipped in the gravy and Rodriguez ordered a regular with sweet peppers and provolone. We each got some of the hand cut fries and a Coke, and extra napkins. I was in heaven.

We were all set at a table by the window, and soon ate enough to satiate our hunger.

Rodriguez took a breath and said, "You know, I think Koz has a point, you might look better with one of those masks."

"Now you too," I said.

She smiled. "Just a thought. Seriously though, I will feel better when they pick up those kids from Englewood. They're like loose cannons out there, and we know that they are young and dumb and have the balls to come north and gang bang people in the middle of the day."

I wasn't sure she was right about that. "They won't be stupid enough to come after us if they can even find us."

"Don't be so sure," she said, "but I hope you're right." She gave herself the sign of the cross.

Frontera Grill on North Clark was our next stop. It is a Mexican themed restaurant opened in Chicago by Chef Rick Bayless that became the flagship in a fleet of new restaurants around the city, some of which did not survive the virus.

We had received a tip overnight that victim number three had been in the restaurant within the last few weeks. Rodriguez knew the place and we went there as it was getting ready to open for dinner. We were looking for a bartender named Diane Fiala. She was at the bar setting up. Rodriguez made the introductions and thanked her for calling.

Diane said she was pretty sure she had served our victim number three at the bar with an older man a few weeks ago.

She described her as a young slender but curvy Asian woman with long straight black hair that sounded like the victim, but the man she described was not our George Clooney, he was not much taller than her and had a gray beard.

I showed Diane a picture I had taken from the security screen from the Godfrey of Clooney and victim three from my phone.

She said, "Oh yeah that's her, without a doubt, but that's definitely not the guy she was with."

"You remember whether they paid with a credit card?" I asked.

She smiled and looked and shook her head. "He left me a $50 tip for two margaritas. I think he was trying to impress the lady."

We thanked Diane, returned to the car and took our places.

When we got back to the station, I went to my car and picked up my report for Whitehead that I had written late last night. I brought it over to the Lieutenant's office along with my discharge from Northwestern Memorial. I knocked on his door which was open, and he waved me in. I put the papers on his desk. He noted that it was late. I started to respond and he said that he didn't have time and told me to check in with Sergeant Simpson.

I went back to the detectives' room where now the whole task force had gathered. I was the last one to arrive so I sat at my desk and listened as Detective Sergeant Clyde Simpson started with a report on what he and Detective Stone had learned at the London House. They were able to view the video from the day and evening before she was found dead in a room that she had booked under the name Sheila Mackenzie. Her credit card confirmed that was her real name and that she was 24 and lived in Villa Park, west of the city. She had checked in at 3:00 p.m. and had three male visitors, each for approximately an hour. Two of the guys entered her room wearing facemasks, including the last guy who also wore a Fedora. They were trying to identify the first two men but were more focused on the last guy for obvious reasons. He had entered the room a little after 8:00 p.m. and left a little before 9:00 p.m., wearing a black surgical mask, a black full-length overcoat and black pants. He was about 5'11" or 6' white, and looked like he had dark brown or black hair. His eyes appeared to be gray or steel blue. He went directly to the elevators on the eighth floor and then was seen getting off on the main floor and walking directly out onto Wacker Drive. From there he turned east toward the lake, before disappearing from view. Simpson said they were trying to find more cameras on that street but they'd had no luck so far. They did confirm that Sheila Mackenzie was working as an escort after finding her ad on the A-list website, a well-known site, advertising escort services. She was using the name Ruby Red. The Medical Examiner verified that she was strangled to death, seemingly with bare hands. The toxicology was not in yet.

The other detectives investigating victims one and three had similar stories.

Baker and Kozlowski studied the video from the Peninsula and observed victim number one's activity on the two days before she was found dead in her room. She had checked in under her real name of Leticia Rice, an athletic 22-year-old black girl from Kenwood. She had also been advertising escort services on the A-list as Brown Sugar. Because there had not been obvious signs of a struggle, her death was not initially determined to be a homicide. However, the Medical Examiner had now determined that she was suffocated to death, probably with a pillow and possibly after being doped up. They had done a tox screen on her because they could not determine the cause of death with a cursory exam. The autopsy later showed evidence of suffocation including bloodshot eyes and mild bruising around her nose and mouth. She was also found to have a large amount of Benadryl in her system, probably not enough to kill a healthy young person but enough to knock her out.

She had checked in on Wednesday and had a couple of visitors that day and four on Thursday. The last guy was wearing a blue gator pulled over his mouth and nose, a blue Cubs baseball hat, and a navy-blue squall jacket and loose-fitting blue jeans. He looked to be about 5'11" or 6' and of average build.

Ladner and Sanchez had a similar story concerning number three at the Ritz who checked in on Monday and was found with an ice pick in her right eye Tuesday morning. She had booked three nights and had two visitors. Monday, the second visitor came to her room at 7:00 p.m. and left at 7:50 p.m.

Monday was cold and blustery, and he came in wearing the same type of long black overcoat as the man last seen coming out of Sheila Mackenzie's room. He was also wearing charcoal slacks, a black knit cap and a black scarf pulled over his mouth and nose. This time he also was wearing black gloves. He was estimated to be about 6' and looked to be of average build.

As was the same as with the other two times, he left the room and went directly to the elevators and then to the main floor and out onto Pearson Street.

Simpson left and reported to Lieutenant Whitehead to get him up to speed.

Rodriguez and I walked out to the officers' parking area and I told my partner that she should meet me here tomorrow at 8:00 a.m. for our trip to Milwaukee.

We decided not to make an appointment with Kotler, it would be better for our meeting to be a surprise. A detective from Milwaukee PD was going to meet us at Kotler's office building at 9:30 a.m.

She got into her red Jeep Wrangler and I slid gingerly into my Camaro. It seemed like a long day and I was still sore in several places. I picked up a Polish and fries and a Coke at Byron's hot dog stand on Irving Park Road and took it home for a quiet night, which it was going to be, subject to an ice pack and an early bedtime.

Chapter 4

Thursday morning was overcast and cold. I arrived at my place of employment, wearing a navy-blue wool blazer, navy slacks, a white shirt, and a red tie with light blue stripes.

Rodriguez had beaten me to work again and looked sharp in a chocolate brown pantsuit and a bright yellow shirt. She wore very little makeup and used a copper brown lip gloss which brings a subtle highlight to her light brown complexion. I needed to push that to the back of my mind and start to concentrate on the job at hand.

I was feeling much better. The swelling on my temple was way down and hardly noticeable and my blackeye was now a crescent shaped ribbon of purple. The scrape on my left knee was healing, and actually only caused discomfort when I bent my leg. Overall, I felt ready for anything.

We checked a few messages and signed out the same Chevy Impala we had driven the day before. The situation was relatively quiet when we left the station, only Del Signore, and Schmid were in the detective room sorting through the tips that came in the previous night. We got in the Impala and Rodriguez drove up to North Avenue and then west to the Kennedy Expressway to head north to Milwaukee. I figured that this would be a good opportunity to get to know my new partner a little better.

Chicagoans identify strongly with the area of the city that they grew up in. If you ask somebody from Chicago where they are from you get one of three answers, West Side, South Side, or North Side. It then gets broken down by neighborhoods.

I knew that Elaina Rodriguez was from the South Side and the Pilsen neighborhood. I have always considered Pilsen to be the South Side but the exact place where the West Side and South Side start is a bit vague. Cermak Road runs right through the center of Pilsen and for some Chicagoans that is the demarcation line. I have always placed the line a little farther north closer to Roosevelt Road. I decided to try a little experiment, so I asked her if she liked baseball.

"Of course!" she exclaimed with gusto.

"Cool, who's your favorite player?" I asked, knowing that this would tell me whether she was a White Sox or Cubs fan.

She was clearly getting a little excited. Her voice rose in her Spanish accent and started becoming more prominent. For the first time with me she spoke a full sentence in Spanish, exclaiming that, "Eloy Jimenez el es magnifico!" Turned out she loves the White Sox.

I winced for two reasons, first I am a huge Cubs fan and second, the Cubs traded Eloy to the White Sox a few years earlier before he had become a star.

I wanted to pursue my theory a little further.

"Who do most of the people in Pilsen root for?" I asked.

She looked at me incredulously. "The Chicago White Sox," she said along with something in Spanish.

I laughed and said, "Okay, I get it. I was just curious. I have never been to Pilsen."

"You are really missing something!" she exclaimed. "I will have to take you there. You have to hear the music, see the art and taste the food."

"I would like that," I said. "I hope you will still have my back even though I am a Cubs fan."

"No problem," she said then she laughed and added, "except on the days when we play the Cubs."

Chicago baseball fans are used to the banter back and forth between Cubs and White Sox fans. It is mostly good-natured and runs pretty true along the South and North Sides with respective suburbs following; the West Side, however, is a little different.

I am 29 years old and grew up in Gale Wood and went to Fenwick High School which is located in Oak Park. The first western suburbs start at Austin Boulevard where the last West Side neighborhood ends coming directly west from downtown. Most of my friends and I were Cub fans. We went to Wrigley Field. We fell in love with the vine covered brick walls, and its history and the cool neighborhood of Wrigleyville. But that wasn't always the case with my father's generation, and my grandfather's generation mostly had been White Sox fans.

As we left the Kennedy Expressway in favor of the Eden's, I started to tell Elaina a little family history. She is a very good listener and seemed genuinely interested. My family is fourth generation in Chicago on my father's side. My great-grandfather Eamon came to the U.S. in 1895 at the age of six and moved to Chicago with his family. In 1903 he started working at age 14 as a laborer and blacksmith and eventually a machinist in a shoe factory. He was the fifth of 12 children. Four of his older siblings had already died by the time they had moved to the U.S. from Ireland arriving in New York from County Kerry. My grandfather was born in 1924 and went into the Army right out of Austin high school in 1942. That struck a chord with Rodriguez.

She explained she was very proud of her time serving in the Army, and that her grandfather was also in the Army during World War II. He came to Chicago as a teenager in the 30s and got work in the stockyards. He was one of nine kids. He and his younger brother Jesus were the only ones to come here. The family were farmers, but they were dirt poor, and the stockyards gave them a chance. When World War II happened, they both enlisted and were sent to Europe during the invasion. After they returned, they got jobs in the steel mills and moved to Pilsen. "My family has been there ever since," she said.

"Why did you want to transfer out of there?" I asked.

"I didn't like walking down the street and running into people that I had arrested. My girls are two and four and don't really know any better, but I want to stay living there. It took me a year but I'm glad to be at the Near North."

We left the Eden's Expressway and merged onto Illinois Tollway Interstate 94. "We'll have to check out a Cubs-Sox game," she said. and I nodded. "Sounds like a good idea."

She turned the focus to the case. "Do you know anybody at Milwaukee PD?" she asked.

"Not really," I responded, "I went to a conference up there a few years ago but mainly hung out with the Chicago PD guys that I work with. It should be fine. We won't talk about football."

We used GPS to get into downtown and were directed to the Milwaukee Center Office Tower on East Kilburn Ave. We found a parking lot nearby and took a short walk to a striking building of cement, brick and glass. We walked in the front door and stepped into a spacious rotunda decorated in black and white, shiny tile floors, high ceilings and arches. My phone buzzed. It was

34

Lieutenant Whitehead. He told me that a Detective Hauser will be there to accompany us to meet with Richard Kotler.

Rodriguez walked over to the Security Desk and asked the guard if she knew Richard Kotler.

The guard nodded and said, "His office is on the ninth floor, he works for a tech firm that has most of the ninth and tenth floors."

Just then a tall blonde guy with a gray suit and short cropped hair and straight posture walked into the rotunda and straight toward us.

He stopped when he got a few feet from us and asked, "Fallon and Rodriguez?" Elaina handled the introductions. He asked if we informed them and that we had not made an appointment. He said we were welcome to use a room at the Milwaukee PD if we needed to.

We thanked him and I said, "That would be great, we'll see how it goes."

We took the elevator up to the ninth floor. The reception area was very modern and had a black-and-white color scheme. The waiting room featured several slick black chairs and a glass topped coffee table with silver legs. We approached the receptionist and asked to see Mr. Kotler. We told her who we were, and she asked if we had an appointment.

We told he that we did not but that it was important and it was official business.'

She picked up the phone and spoke briefly to Kotler then excused herself and walked down the hallway to our left and disappeared into an office. Five minutes later she came out and said, "Mr. Kotler needs to finish up with a phone call and will be with you in a little while."

We sat down in the waiting area and talked with Detective Harry Hauser for a while. He seemed like a good guy and the subject of the Packers never came up.

After about 15 minutes Richard Kotler walked out of his office and down the hall to the waiting area. He introduced himself and politely told us that it took him a while to get a hold of his attorney and he had been advised not to talk to us. He handed us a business card with his lawyer's name and number on it. He said that he was sorry that we came all the way from Chicago but that we could talk to Laura Kopecky, his attorney. He turned and walked back down the hall.

We got up and exited the waiting area and headed to the elevators. On the way down, we thanked Hauser and we walked back to our car and took our places.

Elaina looked at me and asked, "Would you like to drive?"

I said, "No, I'm kind of enjoying being the passenger. Maybe next time."

We pulled out into the street and set the GPS so that we could find our way back to the highway.

"What did you think of Kotler?" I asked.

"I think he has dark hair, gray eyes and is around six feet tall. I'd like to know where he was the nights that the victims were killed."

"Yeah, he looks like he could be about the right size. He didn't even ask why we wanted to talk to him, that's a little odd."

On the ride back, Elaina and I exchange more family history and generally got to know each other a little better. Partnerships on a police force are extremely important and can be tricky. I was lucky to have had Vernon Johnson and now I was feeling pretty good about Elaina Rodriguez.

When we got back in the city, we exited the Kennedy Expressway and Elaina drove to a delicatessen on West Erie. It was a little after noon and we were both hungry. We went in and ordered sandwiches to go. I got pastrami with Swiss and deli mustard and Rodriguez got the roast beef with cheddar, tomato and lettuce. We had some chips and pop and we were on our way back to the station.

When we arrived, most of the detectives were out except detectives Baker and Kozlowski. They had been down to Englewood to talk to the victim Leticia Rice's family. It turned out that Leticia had been living at home with her mother and two younger brothers in a tidy apartment in the Englewood neighborhood. They had reported her missing after she didn't come home three weeks ago. She was finishing her college degree at Chicago State. They thought she was working at a 7-11 in Hyde Park. They were devastated by her death and totally shocked that she was working as an escort.

We spent the rest of the afternoon reviewing tips and making phone calls and tracking down the viable ones. Nothing of much interest materialized except that it turned out that the other two victims also came from caring families and were well educated.

Janelle Park had done a year of graduate school in psychology and was escorting to make enough money to continue her studies. There was no

36

indication that the women knew one another. They were in some ways from completely different worlds. Yet in essence, they were identical twins. I had to wonder if there was a pattern or a connection. I decided to wrap up my day at 5:45. I told Rodriguez I would see her in the morning and said my goodbyes to the rest of the team Most of them had returned the favor. Koz grunted, but otherwise acted human.

On the way home I called a couple of friends and organized a little get together for later. I also decided to stop by the Jewel Grocery Store on North Sheridan Road to get some much-needed food and supplies for my apartment. It took a while since I was still getting used to a new store and there were a lot of things to buy.

At home I made myself a cheeseburger and fries and put on the last of the early evening news. I was enjoying the nighttime city views from my apartment and starting to relax a little when I heard something that almost made me choke on my food. Richard Kotler's picture was on the TV and he was being described as a person of interest in the slaying of Janelle Park at the Ritz-Carlton, and possibly two other women at Near North hotels in the past three weeks. I was thinking *oh, crap, no one is ever going to talk to us now!*

I put down my cheeseburger and called Rodriguez, "Elaina, have you been watching the news?"

She said, "Yeah, how the hell did this get out? I was going to call you after I finished having dinner with Paco and the kids."

"This sure won't make Kotler and his lawyer happy," I said stating the obvious. "We'll have to call the lawyer tomorrow," Elaina added.

"Okay," I said, "see you then."

I had decided to meet up with some buddies at the Gaslight, a bar and grill on Clark Street in Lincoln Park. It is a place I started hanging out at while in college at DePaul. Some of my teammates from DePaul's basketball team and I went there for the sports and the good bar food.

We knew that the Cubs game would be on so it was a natural place to go. I got there at 7:30 and Bill Grimes, an old friend from Fenwick, was already there. We played basketball together at Fenwick High and still played together sometimes on some men's league teams.

I joined him at the bar and ordered a Miller from a young dark-haired woman named Dori. I had seen her before but I didn't really know her. It was good to catch up with Billy, I hadn't seen him since I moved to Uptown. He works downtown at PMO Harris Bank and has been living in Lincoln Park for about a year with his girlfriend Carrie. He knows Gina and my relationship with her and asked me how I was doing.

I said, "Honestly, I miss her a lot but I can't really give her what she wants and needs. I'm not ready to get married and have kids. You know, the whole catastrophe."

Just then another friend, Jogi Kiagi walked into the bar. We went to DePaul together and he has also known Grimes for several years. He is a lawyer at Baker and Mackenzie in their large international division and is married with a little girl and lives in the West Loop. He has fully embraced the total catastrophe. His wife Debbie is also a lawyer and I asked how she and the two-year-old Amanda were doing, and he reported that all was well.

We settled in for some stories about work and old times and a few more beers and by 10:00, the stories had petered out and the Cubs had lost a close one.

We paid up, said good night to Dori and walked out the door to Clark Street. The night was brisk but the skies had cleared and it felt invigorating. I said my goodbyes to the guys and got into my Camaro and drove east on Fullerton toward the Lake and got on Lakeshore Drive heading north. The dichotomy between the quiet darkness of the vast inland ocean of Lake Michigan on my right and the light filled buildings reaching up to the sky illuminating the sprawling city of Chicago to my left was stunning. Somehow, I love them both. I had been familiar with the Lake my whole life but I was feeling like I was just getting to know it for the first time. The great city had always been fascinating to me, fantastical, exciting and coldly unforgiving. On this night I concentrated on the tranquility in the dark, quiet serenity of the Lake.

Chapter 5

On Friday morning I was awakened at seven by a phone call from Elaina. She was already at the station working the tip line and was kind of excited about one of them. She was in early because she and her family go to Mass on Good Friday evening and then have a solemn observance at home. We were both Catholic, but I couldn't help thinking how different it was for her family and mine. She went to the public schools in Pilsen, including Benito Juarez high school, and my family had been sending their kids to Catholic schools for generations but it seemed clear that Elaina's family was more devout. We were sent to the Catholic schools in recent generations, more for practical than religious reasons.

I agreed to hustle down to the station and hopped out of bed. To my surprise and chagrin, one look out the window told me that the weather had shifted overnight and the skies were full of wet snow. No time for breakfast today, just time to shave and shower. A gray suit and black long overcoat matched the weather, and I was off to work.

I was able to get to the station by 7:45 and Rodriguez and Simpson were the only task force members in the room. I took off my snow-covered overcoat and sat down next to Rodriguez.

She slid an intake sheet in front of me and said, "Take a look at this."

It was a tip that came in late last night and written down by the night desk sergeant. The tipster was listed as an anonymous male but there was a phone number that came up on the caller ID. She said, "The message was that this person knew of a group of women that he thinks might be at risk from someone killing escorts in Chicago. He said that he doesn't want his name to become public because he is married and has a professional relationship with some of these women. He said that if he can be assured of anonymity, he will give us more specific information. He wants us to call him on the burner phone he called from."

I looked at Elaina and said, "That's weird, he wants us to protect his favorite escorts. I think he's a wacko."

Elaina wasn't so sure.

"Maybe," she said, "he could be the wacko that's killing these women and wants to insert himself into the investigation, and even if he is harmless, if this group of escorts exists, they might have heard something or even run across our perp. I think we should give him a call."

We decided to use one of the interrogation rooms. We found an empty room, went in and closed the door. Rodriguez put her phone on the table before dialing the number and putting it on speaker.

She turned to me and said, "You're looking better today, Jack. You must be a fast healer."

I replied, "I had to be, with an older brother and older cousins." Elaina laughed and said, "I know how that goes."

She punched in the numbers and we listened to a symphonic ring back tone.

That was soon replaced by the deep bass voice of a man on the line. Elaina introduced herself and informed him that he was on speaker and that I would also be in the room. She then asked him if he could tell us who he is.

He replied, "Not at this time."

After telling him that was okay for now, she then asked, "What can you share with us?"

There was a long pause before he spoke again.

"Okay, this may all seem unbelievable at first, but hear me out. I am a financial advisor. I'm not blowing smoke, but I deal with large investments and high-end clients. A few years ago one of my clients, who has extensive business and investments in Europe, introduced me to an attractive woman named Sophie. Before I go any further, I want to know that you will not go after me or anyone I tell you about on any kind of vice charges. I need to hear that from both of you. I am recording this and I assume you are doing the same."

Rodriguez muted the phone and looked at me with her piercing brown eyes. "What do you want to do?" she asked.

"We're talking about murders here. We're talking about a possible serial killer here. I'm not worried about what those people do in private as long as there are no children involved in anything and it is consensual. I am not looking to jail anybody here except the killer."

Elaina nodded, and unmuted the phone. "Are you still there?" she asked. We heard the same deep voice. "Yeah, I'm here."

"My partner and I have talked about what your current concern is and we get it and we agree. We will not pursue any charges against you or anyone you tell us about as long as there are isn't any underage or forced participants. Also of course, any violent felonies or gun charges will be pursued."

I chimed in and assured our tipster that I was fully on board. There was another long pause.

"Okay, I will trust you guys on this. I am only telling you these things because I genuinely care about some people that I think could be at risk. As I was saying, I have this client who is also a friend and who knows that I occasionally enjoy the company of professional sex workers, you know, escorts. So, a few years ago he was in Europe on business and well, let's just say he has some of the same hobbies that I do."

He laughed and said, "He also plays golf."

If we were supposed to respond, we didn't. He continued. "Anyway, he was in Vienna, staying at a five-star hotel and he asked the concierge if he could hook him up. The concierge said he would see what he can do. A few euros changed hands and half an hour later the phone in his room rang. The concierge told him that he had found what he was looking for and that it would be arranged in an hour. He didn't mention a price and my friend didn't ask what the going rates were, and believe me, he can afford it.

"So, he meets this gorgeous Austrian woman, and he stays in touch with her. He sees her a few times in Vienna. She lets him know that she has friends in the States and she would love to introduce them to him.

"Now this guy lives in Chicago and often travels to New York. Before you know it, he has a bunch of new friends and he's loving it. These women work only on referrals. They don't advertise or promote themselves in any way. They are all professional women who are here legally. Some of them won the immigration lottery, others came in on work or student visas and worked their way to green cards and citizenship. They are all Austrians who met in Vienna at the University.

"I was introduced to Sophie and have gotten to know her and several of the other women who are mainly based in Chicago. They travel mainly between Chicago and New York and Las Vegas but they could go anywhere with friends. Sometimes he will take one of them with him on business trips. They are expensive and everything is first class. They are all attractive but most of all charming and sexual and sensual. Nothing is ever rushed or uncomfortable. You can tell I like them."

We didn't say a word. No need to interrupt since he seemed to be on a roll. "The reason I called you guys is that when the story came out about Richard Kotler being a suspect or person of interest or whatever, I kind of freaked out because I don't know this guy that well but he is a friend of the guy who introduced me to these ladies and I don't know what to do about it. I didn't know for sure if Kotler has been one of their customers and Sophie won't tell me. They never talk about their clients and I don't want to ruin my relationship with them by pushing the questioning too far. They are on the same level and go to the same high-end hotels as the women who have been murdered. I am worried that they are at risk and that they may have helpful information. They may have even dealt with this guy."

Elaina blinked and looked at me before saying, "That's quite a story. Tell me, do you have phone numbers and addresses for these women?"

"I have general phone numbers but I'm not sure where they are living right now. They move around every year or two. Approaching them directly won't work. As police officers you can't even approach them for a meeting. Someone would have to refer you."

"Would you be willing to do that for us?" I asked.

"I will have to think about it, Can I call this number you are on now?"

Elaina replied, "Yes, ask for Detective Rodriguez, just don't call this weekend, it is Easter."

I interrupted and said, "You can call me anytime," and recited my phone number. He said, "Thanks for listening to my story. I will get in touch with you."

Elaina hung up. "Does this all sound believable to you?" she asked.

I said, "I'm not sure. I would like to know who this guy is and what he looks like."

"Yeah, maybe six feet tall with dark hair. Yeah, I wonder. Let's give Richard Kotler's lawyer a call." I dialed Laura Kopecky's number and put it on speaker. I got the reception desk and was soon connected to Attorney Laura Kopecky. She was made aware that she was on speaker with myself and Detective Rodriguez.

She said that was fine and asked how she could help us? "Well, you can start by allowing us to talk to a client." There was a pause and a laugh.

"Well, exactly what would you like to talk to him about?"

"We'd like to know about his relationships with Janelle Park and possibly others."

She responded, rather coldly, that they were not admitting that he had a relationship with Ms. Park or anyone else.

"We have a video of him having drinks with her at the Godfrey Hotel," I said equally coldly.

"Sure, we can agree that he had a drink with her at the Godfrey, so what?"

"Listen," I said, "let's not waste each other's time here. We know what was going on and we know Kotler is a frequent flyer with escorts, including Janelle Park."

Kopecky quickly retorted, "Then you would also know why I might not want my client to answer questions about alleged illegal behavior without the promise of immunity."

It was my turn to laugh. "That seems to be a popular request to us today." I looked at Rodriguez and she nodded. I said, "We can guarantee we will not be looking to hang any vice charges on your client as long as he is not involved in any violent crimes or gun related crimes as long as he is truthful with us."

"That's great!" Kopecky exclaimed, "send me a letter from the State's Attorney's office and I will discuss it with my client."

I frowned and said something to Rodriguez, expressing what I thought of Kopecky's demand. I then told her that I would see what I could do about that, but it would take until next week before I could get back to her.

She said that was fine since it was her understanding that Kotler was going to be out of town for the Easter weekend anyway.

We went back to the detectives' room and began sifting through more tips. All of the task force members were there. By noon there were no major breaks in the case and no direct links between the victims could be established.

Someone ordered a couple of thin crust pizzas and everybody had some along with coffee or pop. As it turned out Rodriguez wasn't the only one with Good Friday plans and a few of the detectives left right after lunch and the rest filed out one by one. By three, Rodriguez and I were the last ones left. We decided to call it a day. She was on her way to get her family ready for Mass and I decided to go to the gym.

I pulled my Camaro out of the officers' parking lot and before long I was pulling it into the Member Lot at the Lakeview YMCA on North Marshfield Ave. I had joined the Lakeview Y in February shortly after moving to Uptown and tried to get a workout of some kind two or three times a week. I got my gym bag out of the trunk and looked up at this classic old school Y building. It had stopped snowing a couple of hours earlier and most of the snow had melted off the pavement and was dripping off the trees. Just another April day in Chicago. The Y is like others I have been in around Chicagoland. It had rooms for rent and a small pool area, a basketball court and workout room. I changed in the somewhat cramped but functional locker room and went to the gym. The court was open and I decided to shoot around for a while to kind of get warmed up for my league game the next morning. I felt pretty good as banged up as I had been a few days earlier. I was looking forward to tomorrow. We were in the semi-finals and everybody on the team was psyched up for it. After 20 minutes of shooting, I went to the weight room and did some light repetitions with 20-pound weights and used a couple of the machines. I hit the showers and by the time I got back in my car it was around 4:30.

On my way home Morgan Latner called to see if I wanted to go out later. He was having dinner with his mom in Evanston and then would be free.

I said, "Sure, there's a place in my neighborhood that I've been meaning to try called the Green Mill on Broadway and Lawrence, let's meet there at eight."

He said, "Okay, I'll see you there."

Later that evening the skies had cleared and the weather was actually getting a little warmer, so I decided to walk. It's less than a mile from my apartment to the Green Mill. I put on a navy cotton sweater and blue jeans, sneakers and a midweight royal blue squall jacket. I like walking and have always walked around my neighborhood wherever I have lived since I was a little kid.

I walked up North Clarendon Avenue to Lawrence Avenue crossed the street and turned left to walk west on Lawrence. In a few minutes I got to North Broadway, crossed the street, turned north and there it was on the left. I realized that I had told Latner that the place was on the corner, but it was close enough, he'd figure it out. The Green Mill was lit up with a bright neon sign announcing the Green Mill Cocktail Lounge. It is very old-school with a history of jazz musicians and colorful characters which included Al Capone among them.

44

Sure enough, Latner had found the place and was already at the bar. I joined him with a high five and looked around the half-full establishment. The decor was eclectic and a mixture of colors and styles that was somehow between quaint and gaudy. A Jazz Trio was finishing up the early show. The small stage was surrounded by tables and a piano pressed right up to its base, and a bright lit up sign with green script saying Green Mill.

I didn't quite know what to make of the place but I decided that I liked it.

Everything seemed to move slowly in a super relaxed atmosphere. Our bartender, a 50 something guy, with a gray goatee, and a colorful knit hat, got up from one of the small round tables where he had been sitting down with a couple of customers and ambled over behind the bar.

"What can I do you for gents?"

We ordered a couple of bottles of beer and a couple of shots. He came back with my Miller and a bottle Coors light for Latner. He poured a couple of healthy shots of Jack Daniels into small rocks glasses and declined when I asked him if he would like one; he said it was a little early for him. I definitely got the feeling that this was a real late-night place. I said to myself that was for another time. I wanted to be in decent shape for tomorrow's game.

The bartender introduced himself as Gus Kezios, He had been bartending there for 20 years and had been a patron before that. Previously, he had worked for years as a union carpenter, but gave that up after his kids left the house. Turns out he was in his 60s and was also a West Sider from Austin and then Berwyn. He now lived in Uptown about a mile west of the Mill and liked the neighborhood.

More people started coming in and he seemed to know everybody. Latner and I talked a little bit about the task force and a lot about the Cubs. He was also a big fan of the Cubs and especially in April fans are always optimistic. I could see and feel that this was not the place to watch the Cubs or sports of any kind. No television but this was a cool funky place. I had my sports bars.

I asked Latner if he knew much about our opponents for tomorrow's game since we hadn't played them before. It was a team that normally played in a different division on Thursday nights.

He said that he knew a couple of their players from Park Ridge and Skokie and that they were good, He said they would be bigger than us, but he didn't think they were as fast. We had a couple more rounds and by 9:30 the place was filling up.

Just then a beautiful young woman somewhere in her mid to late 20s confidently walked in and went to the end of the bar and took the last seat. She placed her overcoat over the seat, revealing a voluptuous body even under a turtleneck sweater and jeans. I felt like I was hit by the proverbial lightning bolt. She had this sweet girl next door face with strawberry blonde shoulder length hair and looked like she was about five foot two. She had an air of sensuality and mystery about her. I was hooked and I hadn't even met her.

I waited for Gus to come over. I asked if he knew the young woman.

He said, "Sure, that's Emma. She works here sometimes as an MC or even does a stand-up comedy routine once in a while."

"I asked if he knew if she was married or attached."

He said he didn't think so, but he really wasn't sure. "She has a lot of friends and comes and goes," he said, adding, "you know she's an artist and has the free spirit to match."

I asked if he would introduce me.

He said, "If she wants to meet you, she'll let you know. If you want my advice, take it slow."

I said, "Okay, can you ask her if I can buy her a drink?"

He smiled and said, "I'll ask," then went to the end of the bar and spoke to her. I couldn't hear what he said due to the jazz music being played by a second group on the stage now and a guy playing the piano. I could see her look at me, smile and say something to Gus. He brought her some kind of a martini and she took a sip without giving me another look. I had the urge to walk over to her but something told me not to.

Morgan and I had one more beer before paying up and putting on our coats. Emma broke off a conversation with the guy at her end of the bar, got up and walked toward us. My heart jumped into my throat.

She walked right up to me and said, "Hi, I'm Emma."

I wasn't sure what my name was. I had a hard time saying anything. She offered her hand and I took it gently. Her touch sent an electrical wave through me. I was stunned by the experience. I got my name out and didn't bother to introduce Latner.

I kind of stammered. "Can I call you sometime?" I asked.

She smiled slyly and said, "Come by again when you can stay longer." "I'd like that, when are you here?"

She smiled and simply said, "I'm here when I'm here, you will have to find me." She turned and walked away from me and she looked just as good walking away as she did walking toward me.

I hadn't felt anything like this since I'd first met Gina years ago. Latner tugged my arm and tried to snap me out of the spell I was under. I reluctantly broke off my gaze at Emma.

She had resumed her conversation and I was envious of the guy who had her attention. We walked out of the Green Mill into the cool moist air. It was kind of a slap in the face which sort of snapped me out of it. Morgan was parked nearby and offered to give me a ride home but I felt like the walk would be good for me. I started to cross Lawrence and it was clear I was still thinking about Emma and wasn't really paying attention to my surroundings. I didn't notice the two young black men in a dark SUV parked on the south side of Lawrence with the engine running and no headlights. When I got to the middle of the street the parked car charged out onto the road with no lights and screeching tires. I reacted and took two long strides toward the curb and jumped toward the sidewalk. The dark SUV was on me so fast that I couldn't believe it. It narrowly missed me. They overshot me by about 30 feet and stopped and started backing up. At that moment Latner drove up and stopped in the middle of Lawrence Avenue blocking the path of the SUV. He got out and leveled a gun at the car. That stopped them and they sped off toward the Lake.

I picked myself up off the sidewalk and said, "Thanks, man, those jagoffs tried to kill me."

This time I gladly accepted Morgan's ride home. We called in a report but we only had a vague description of the dark SUV, the two young black men and one letter of the license plate. I had a pretty good idea of who they were, not specifically, but I felt sure it was related to the mugging incident and charges.

I felt like I needed to tell Rodriguez. I called her from home and woke her up. I apologized and told her what had happened. I wanted her to be aware of it and know that she could be a target too. She thanked me and after making sure I was okay simply said, "Good night, Jack."

"Good night, Elaina," I replied.

Chapter 6

Not much rattles me but I woke up after a restless night still a little shaken by the events of the previous evening. I wasn't sure what was more upsetting, the fact that I was now pretty sure I was a target for a hit or that I was completely blown away by a young woman named Emma.

Rodriguez called just to make sure that I was okay and Ricky Del Signore called to see if I would pick him up for the basketball game. He lived in the Loyola neighborhood not far from the field house where we played. He grew up in West Rogers Park and that was the main reason we decided to play in that league. His car was in the shop. The game was at 11, so I told him to be ready at 10:15. I put together a hearty breakfast of crispy bacon, scrambled eggs with cheese and onions, toast, and chocolate milk. I started to feel a little better after breakfast and began to focus on the game.

I put on some music starting with "The 21 Pilots" and started thinking about how the game might go. From what I knew, the team we were playing was full of veteran guys who were a little older and bigger than we were. We had nine players on our team, three detectives, Latner, Del Signore and myself and a few uniformed officers we knew, and a couple of their friends.

Everyone on the team had played in high school and a couple played at junior colleges, including Latner I was the only guy that played Division I college ball, so I was elected to run the substitutes and basically act as Captain. Everybody played a lot, with Latner and myself playing a little bit more than the rest of the guys. I hit the road around 10 and let Ricky know that I would be on time. He needed to come down to the street from his high-rise apartment which was just south of the main Loyola University Campus just off Sheridan Road. After picking him up it only took a few minutes to get to the gym.

We hustled into the building leaving the chilly gray morning behind us. Latner was there with Nick Eddy, one of the patrolmen from the near North. Soon all the guys got there and we changed into our game gear which included black short-sleeved shirts we had made for us with script in green that said Timothy O'Toole's. My number is 32. We were playing a team called Kearns which is a bar in Edison Park. We walked out onto the gym floor.

In the bleachers there was a group of about 70 people, including our opponents who were watching the finish of the other semifinal game, a team called Swift, wearing green shirts with white letter and numbers, against the first-place team, Levine's Auto in Skokie from the Thursday night league wearing white with maroon numbers and lettering. It ended with Swift losing by 10. They shook hands and we took to the court to warm up.

I had a chance to size up the guys on the other end of the court wearing gold shirts with blue letters and numbers. Yeah, they were pretty big, thicker and wider, with a couple of their guys being taller than our Center Nick Eddy who is 6'6". I also noticed a player that I recognized from other leagues I had been in over the years. His name is Jackie Gilchrist, and he is a stud, is around 6'2" and a built like an NFL running back. In fact, he has an uncle who played running back for the New York Giants. I knew that I would have to guard him throughout much of the game and I also knew from previous experience that I would have my hands full.

The refs walked in and I recognized one of them. A middle-aged guy that I have dealt with in several other leagues and in a few of our games this year. I wasn't a big fan, and he didn't like me either. He once had me thrown out of a game that he had allowed to start by letting me take the court while I was on crutches for the opening jump because we only had four guys that were ready to play and you need five to start. I had a severely sprained ankle from the week before and couldn't walk without crutches so when the jump ball went up and the game started it was halted as soon as possible. With clock stopped, I was allowed to leave the floor. Shortly thereafter I sat down on the team bench and he made a terrible call which he was prone to do and I let him know what I thought of the call. He stopped the game and went ballistic and kicked me out not only of the game but the gym building. I figured that I was just going to have to deal with it.

The captains were called out to talk to the refs. I said hi and shook hands with Jackie and the refs. The ref that I knew scowled at me and all I could do was think ok here we go. We huddled up and I mentioned to the guys that I knew the ref and warned against bitching about the calls. Sure enough, early in the game we had a missed shot and Kearns came back at us on a fast break.

49

We had quickly reacted and got back on defense. One of their forwards passed the ball up to Jackie Gilchrist who caught it on the run and I could see that he had already decided to take it all the way to the basket. I cut him off and had perfect position to take the charge. I was stationary about seven feet from the basket on the left side of the lane. He buried his right shoulder into the middle of my chest and I went flying backward sliding all the way out of bounds with Jackie on top of me and the ball rolling out of bounds over the sideline. I looked up to see my buddy the ref, standing over me and yelling out "foul" blocking on 32. I jumped up put my hands on my head and the ref stared daggers at me. I held my tongue, just turned away and put it out of my mind.

After that, the game continued sluggishly with neither team shooting well and nobody leading by more than three points. The first half ended with us behind 23-22. The game was physical and chippy. There were a lot of fouls called with Kearns drawing a few more than we did. The second half wasn't much better than the first with just as much fouling and slightly better shooting. Latner and Eddy started getting free for some short-range jump shots. I was having trouble making the few shots that I got but was making my free throws. With just under 30 seconds to go, we got the ball back and called a timeout. We were down 54–53. I told the guys that if we didn't get a layup, we should look for a shot inside of 10 seconds and crash the boards in case the shot missed. I inbounded the ball to Del Signore who gave it back to me. I drove off the screen by Eddy and drew Eddy's man to me. Eddy stepped back and was open for a shot from just inside the key but Latner's man on the wing jumped in to double-team me and the only pass I had was to bounce the ball to Latner to my right as we were running out of time. Latner's man recovered and tried to cut him off but Latner moved quickly to his right before a defender was able to get to him. He pulled up for a 12-foot jump shot with five seconds left.

Everybody followed the ball to the basket. It hit off the far side of the rim and bounced over Nick Eddy and into the hands of one of the Kearn's forwards. The rebound literally fell into his hands while he was facing the basket with his back to me. He turned around right into me holding the ball with two hands near his waist. I pounded down on the ball with my right hand and it came out of his hands off the floor and right to me. My buddy, the ref, was standing right there. He knew it was clean, but his whistle was in his mouth. Thank God there was no call. I flipped the ball to Del Signore a few feet up the wing from me and he immediately passed it to Latner who was just below the free-throw line. Latner didn't hesitate. He jumped and shot from 14 feet. It swished as the horn sounded.

We were stunned and jubilant. We celebrated with high-fives for a minute before settling down to shake hands with the Kearns players. It had been an unusually rough game, but they were good sports. Jackie had a good game but didn't shoot as well as he normally does, which saved us. I shook hands with him and then looked for the ref. I went over to him. He had just put on his jacket and I offered my hand, and he took it and smiled. I said, "thanks" and he smiled and nodded. Perhaps a truce was underway between us.

We showered up and got dressed. We all felt high on the physical adrenaline and emotional satisfaction from winning such a fierce contest. We all agreed to meet at O'Toole's at 3. I wanted to go back to the station first and Del Signore wanted to check in too, so we drove to the district station on North Larabee Street. None of the other task force detectives were there but the desk sergeant mentioned that Baker and Simpson had been there earlier. There were always some detectives on call. Del Signore, Latner and I were not on call that day. We started looking at the tips from that morning and started making some calls to follow up on the most interesting ones. One woman was certain that her ex-husband was the escorts killer. This poor woman said he fit the general description of the suspect and that he was a violent guy who had assaulted her and spent some time in Cook County Jail. The story was checking out right up until I was able to verify that the husband had been living in Seattle and was in the local jail there for the past month. Apparently, he is a real asshole but not our asshole. All of the leads pretty much ended the same way. At 2:45 we wrapped it up and took the short drive to Timothy O'Toole's to catch up with the guys. When we walked in, we were greeted with some exaggerated applause and cheers from Charlie, a waitress named Savon and my brother Barry. The team members were all at tables on the side room with two pitchers of beer in front of them. O'Toole's gives us two pitchers after we win. One if we lose.

The bar was hopping on this Saturday afternoon with the White Sox playing at home and the Bulls game was also on TV. We all exchanged another round of high-fives and everyone seemed to be in a joyful mood. I sat down next to Del Signore and across from Latner.

He looked at me and said, "Hey, man, are you okay with what happened last night?"

I nodded and said, "I'm okay, but I'm taking it more seriously now. Rodriguez tried to warn me to be careful, but I didn't really think those guys would come after me. I am worried about Elaina now too."

Latner said that he had called in an Incident Report last night and made sure that Youngblood and Skinner would see it soon. Savon came by with two more pitchers and took orders for wings, burgers, onion rings and fries.

Barry came over and asked if I was going to be at Dad's tomorrow for Easter. I said that I was and that I was bringing dessert. Barry said, "Great, I'll see you tomorrow." And went back to helping Charlie at the bar which was two deep. By six, our group started filing out. We gave our last congratulations to each other and confirmed that we would see everybody the following Saturday morning for another 11 a.m. game for the league overall championship.

I dropped Del Signore off at his building and decided to stop by Montrose Beach on my way home. I drove into the nearly deserted beach parking area. The darkness had fully enveloped the city and looking out onto the lake from the beach it was nearly pitch black. The weather had turned a bit milder with a light cool breeze coming off the 40° water. I walked along the shoreline with only the lapping sound of the waves on the sandy shore and the occasional bark of the German Shepard that was playing a game of pitch and retrieve with the young woman on the far end of the beach.

I couldn't help thinking what a wild week it had been. It had started out calmly enough with goodbyes and well wishes between me and my old partner Vernon Johnson, and the next day meeting my new partner, Elaina Rodriguez. And then all hell seemed to break loose.

Looking out into the vast dark water, clouds broke, allowing just a sliver of moonlight to pierce the darkness making it appear that there was a bright path on the water heading out into the darkness until fading away. I was wondering where it was leading to, where it was leading me to. Wherever it was I was now getting cold and decided to head home.

Easter morning was bright and mild. I put on khaki slacks, a navy polo shirt and a tan windbreaker. On the way to my dad's house, I stopped by Reuters Bakery on West Grand Avenue to pick up some of their famous coffeecake. One pecan and one cherry. I drove to my dad's house which is situated on a quiet street on the western edge of Gale Wood near Elmwood Park. The driveway was already full so I parked on the street in front of his modest Tudor single-family home. It's the house we had moved to before my freshman year in high school with my mom and dad. Brother Barry was going into his senior year of high school at St. Patrick's and my sister Molly was going into her sophomore year at Trinity High School in River Forest. The house and the street hadn't changed much during those 15 years and that was comforting to me. The dynamics of our family, however, had changed a lot. We all grew up and moved out on our own and five years ago my mom had passed away, leaving Dad alone in the house. I walked through the front door with coffee cakes in hand and was immediately rushed and mugged by Barry's two little boys, Rory four and Ian six.

"Hey, Uncle Jack!" they yelled, as they both tried to jump into my full arms.

I managed to get to the kitchen and put the coffee cakes on the counter. I lifted the boys up, one in each arm and they giggled with delight. I put them down and my sister Molly came into the kitchen to give me a warm hug. We had been close as kids and remained that way even though I didn't see her that much since she started working at Northwestern University in Evanston and moved up there. She was slender with shoulder length light brown hair, a few freckles and a contagious wide smile. She looked more like our mom had with her hazel eyes. Barry and I looked more like Dad with dark hair and gray eyes. Molly was single and didn't have a steady boyfriend at that moment. We were in the same boat as far as that goes. Barry's wife Tammy came into the kitchen next followed by my dad, Ed. I hugged them both.

Dad was looking good and in good spirits. He asked me how I was feeling. He had called me Tuesday night at a time when I looked and felt like crap. He kind of looked me over and said that I didn't look too much worse for wear. I knew that my dad cared a great deal for all of us and had tried to be closer since Mom passed away. He wasn't naturally an emotional man. He had always left that side of things to our mother. He was a criminal defense lawyer and had worked his way up to the First Assistant Public Defender's job. He probably would have had the top job but he never really liked politics and was happy where he was. He still did a lot of trials and enjoyed them.

My dad said, "Let's go to the porch."

He led the way through the TV room to a room that was glassed in and led out to a small, nice backyard that my dad had tried to keep up with the flowers that Mom always planted. The only thing visible on that Easter Sunday was a patch of crocuses on the north side of the yard.

This room had been a small screened in porch which had been expanded and turned into a sunroom with heated tile floors and sliding glass doors on three sides. It was a big investment for my folks at the time, but it quickly became everyone's favorite room. My mom's brother, uncle Don Cogan was sitting at the large dining room table at the center of the room with his daughter, my cousin Claire, her husband Franco Ellis. and their 11-year-old daughter Sophia. We all exchanged greetings and everyone sat down. I sat next to Uncle Don. I had always been close to him and Claire growing up. He was a strong man physically and mentally. He had made a career in the Marines and served at the end of the Vietnam War. After 25 years in the service, he has been working as a doorman at the Intercontinental Hotel on Michigan Avenue for the past 20 years. He enjoyed pointing out the irony of the respective work that my dad and I engaged in. I put them in jail and my dad lets them go he liked to say.

We all had a nice time catching up and having some juice and appetizers of cashews and some assorted cheeses and biscuits.

Molly and I talked for a while in the kitchen, she asked if I had seen or heard from Gina lately.

I replied, "Not in the last couple of weeks."

Molly and Gina went to Trinity for a few years together with Molly being a year older. They played varsity basketball together for a couple of years and became good friends They would often ride to school and practices together since Gina grew up in nearby Elmwood Park. I had always thought Gina was very attractive. She had dark brown hair with olive skin and dark almond shaped eyes. But I never dated her in high school, that came years later after we both finished college and met at an after Midnight Mass Christmas party that some mutual friends of ours gave annually in River Forest. Molly said that she was sorry that it hadn't worked out for me and Gina but that she understood. She herself was fiercely independent and wondered out loud whether she would ever make the total commitment.

My dad came into the kitchen, looked in the oven and pulled out a large roasted leg of lamb and placed it on the top of the oven. The pan was full of juices, roasted potatoes, carrots and onions. I went back out to the sunroom and offered to help Barry and Tammy set the table. I was informed that they had covered it. We had some time so I took the boys out to the backyard to play with the wiffle ball I found and a plastic bat. The boys eagerly followed me out to the yard. It wasn't much of a game. We spent most of our time retrieving the ball after I pitched it and one of the boys occasionally batted it around the yard. After around 15 minutes, the game was dying a natural death and we were mercifully called in for dinner. We all managed to fit into the dining room table and enjoyed a great Easter meal of leg of lamb. It was mom's favorite and my dad had mastered it after her passing. Uncle Don, Barry and Molly had some wine and the rest of us had pop, water or milk. Afterward, the coffeecake was a big hit and we all departed feeling full of good food and good spirits. I felt a strong sense of warmth and contentment. The afternoon was still mild and sunny. It was truly the calm before the storm.

Chapter 7

Monday started inauspiciously. It was partly cloudy and windy. I put on some sweats and a windbreaker and left for a run in the park before work. I crossed Clarendon on West Side Place, ran to North Marine Drive, and crossed into the park and ran south to Wilson Avenue then back toward Clarendon and home. It was only a short run but a good way to get the work day started and after a shower and some oatmeal with maple syrup, I was on my way to the station.

I hadn't put on the TV or radio that morning so when I pulled into the parking lot at work, I was surprised to see the TV trucks and several reporters with camera crews. I literally pushed my way through a cluster of reporters who were all asking me to comment on the newest escort murder. I had no idea, not that I would've answered them even if I did.

Inside the task force room everyone seemed to be on the phone or talking to their partner and looking worried. Elaina beat me there as usual. She could tell that I didn't know what was going on.

I sat down beside her and whispered, "What the hell happened?"

She whispered back, "A young woman was found bound and nailed to her bed at a swanky apartment building on West Illinois Street. Her roommate came home late last night after being away for the weekend. Simpson and Stone are at the scene now. They called homicide first but it seems this might be connected to our murders. The victim was Nina Eisen, age 23. Both she and her roommate, Arielle Katzenberg, were both attractive aspiring models who somehow could afford a $4,000 a month, two-bedroom apartment in River North. The media has put two and two together already, so they have given it to us. Whitehead wants you and me to do the victimology and profile, her roommate as well. They are both from Lincolnwood and went to high school together at Niles West. The roommate was hysterical and taken to Rush University Hospital as a precaution."

Elaina told me to turn on my computer and check my email. She had sent me crime scene photos. The gruesome pictures took my breath away. This young woman had been brutalized and tortured beyond belief. She laid in a dried pool of blood, her body appeared to be painted in dark red and the walls were decorated with a spray of the same. My eyes could not escape being fixated on her head, her hair that had once been platinum blonde, was soaked in blood and ringed with a crown of barbed wire. Her hands were tied to the bed posts with what looked like a neck tie and nailed down to the bed with long large nails as were her feet one on top of the other. Her naked body had been pierced under the ribs with a large kitchen knife that was protruding from her left side. She had a look of absolute terror on her face with her eyes wide open. I clicked it off. How do you show her family something like that? I didn't intend to do that and neither did Elaina, but we had to go and see her parents. We left right away to drive to the nearby northern suburb of Lincolnwood, a nice community nestled in between Chicago and Skokie. We found the parents' house in the middle of a quiet tree-lined street and parked in the driveway. We took the stone walkway to the front door of a nice-looking brick split-level ranch with thick bushes on either side of the door. I pushed the doorbell and a few seconds later the door opened and there stood Paul and Marjorie Eisen, the saddest two parents I could ever remember seeing. We introduced ourselves and gingerly asked if we could come in. Mr. Eisen nodded and they led us into their living room. I imagined family gatherings like the one I had just attended the day before. It was heartbreaking but we had to do our job as terrible as it may be at times. Elaina sensed the bottomless depth of these parents' grief.

She took the mother's hand and looked them both in their bloodshot eyes and simply said, "I am a mother, my heart breaks for you."

The father dropped his head and began whimpering while the mother shook with deep cries of pathetic misery. Elaina took mom's hand and we sat in silence until Mr. Eisen raised his head and was able to get out the words thank you. Mrs. Eisen stopped shaking and her crying became more of a quiet despair than shrieking anguish.

Elaina had made a connection so I let her keep it going. "When was the last time you saw her?"

Mr. Eisen responded, "She was supposed to come to our house for Passover but had a modeling job out of town so we were going to have her home for dinner next weekend. They hadn't seen her since early March."

Elaina asked if they knew very much about her modeling work.

They looked at each other and both said, not really, she had started it about a year earlier after her good friend from high school Arielle introduced her to a modeling agency downtown. They were hoping she would go to law school after graduating with honors from the University of Wisconsin but they said she seemed happy and they felt the neighborhood in River North was safe.

Now Mom was crying again and repeating, "We should have made her go to law school."

Later, Elaina took her hand again and I asked the father if he had the name of the modeling agency that Arielle worked for.

Mr. Eisen said, "It was the Ford Agency on Jackson Boulevard in the West Loop."

We thanked them and I patted Mr. Eisen on the shoulder and said, "We will show ourselves out."

We got into our sedan and Elaina slowly backed the car out of the driveway. It was around 9:30. We decided to go to the agency before going to the hospital to see Arielle.

Before long we were parked in front of the Ford Modeling Agency on West Jackson. It was a well-known agency and one of Chicago's best for high-end fashion. We walked into the window dominated brick building. The lobby was ultramodern chic. We showed our IDs to the young man sitting at reception, dressed in a hip business casual suit and asked if we could speak to someone who would be familiar with Nina Eisen and Arielle Katzenberg.

He punched in something on his computer and told us, "Please take a seat and someone will be with you shortly."

We had just sat down when an elegant woman somewhere in her 50s strode briskly into the lobby from the elevator. She knew who we were and introduced herself as Dorothy St. John, the Director of Modeling Assignments at Ford. She sat down with us and as there was no one else around, she seemed willing to speak to us right there.

"How may I help you?" she asked confidently.

Rodriguez began by relaying our condolences concerning Nina Eisen's horrible murder. She followed that by asking Ms. St. John what she could tell us about the two young women. She smiled a smile that was both disarming and cautionary. It seemed to say 'I am secure enough to be polite to anybody but don't underestimate me.'

She said that the girls had been working off and on for her for about a year. We later learned that she referred to all of the models as her kids or her girls, etc. She said, she was very fond of them and tried very hard to find them modeling assignments.

"So they had been working regularly?" I asked.

When I asked for more details, Ms. St. John flashed that smile again and leaned back.

"I didn't say that. Nina and Arielle are not on the A-list, they just aren't the high-end fashion types. Don't get me wrong, they are lovely. Excuse me if I can't get myself to refer to Nina in the past tense. They were used on commercials and trade shows mainly as the girl next door types or eye candy. Nina had a gig with the Gap for a little while but everything for those two had been short-term."

"So would you expect they could afford to live in a luxury building in River North?" I asked.

"Heavens no," she replied smiling more widely this time. "I'm aware of where they live but frankly, I assumed that they had support from their families. We do keep track of our models' overall health and weight, mainly, and we try to be aware of any sign of substance abuse. Some of the models, girls especially, have problems with diet pills but that mostly happens with the high fashion models that need to be very slender. I'm not aware of any such problems with Nina and Arielle."

"What about relationship problems?"

"None that I know of," Ms. St. John said, "they're good looking, they're young and seemed to be enjoying what Chicago has to offer. They have a lot of friends. We either host or invite them to a lot of social events in this business. They both seem to enjoy the parties."

"Did either have a steady date at these functions?" I asked.

"Now that you mention it, I don't think so. Is there anything else, detectives, I have a meeting in a couple of minutes."

We glanced at each other and Elaina said, "No. Thanks for your help. Can we call if we think of something?"

She gave us that knowing smile and said, "Certainly my dear. You have a very photogenic face." She handed Elaina her card and said, "If you ever want to get a portfolio going, give me a call, and if you will be talking to Arielle sometime soon, please tell her that we are here for her."

In fact, she was our next stop. It was a short drive to Rush University Medical Center on West Harrison. We discussed our strategy and we decided to address the proverbial elephant in the room with Arielle but we needed to be tactful. We walked into the imposing concrete structure on Harrison Street that is Rush University Medical Center. We got directions to Arielle's room and took the elevator to the third floor. We stopped at the nursing station and asked if Arielle was getting better? She was now mildly sedated and would probably be discharged after the doctor's next visit with her according to the nurse at the desk. We knocked on the open door of Arielle's room and stepped in. I was glad to see that the second bed in the room was empty and Arielle was sitting up watching TV. It was striking to me how young and innocent she looked. I could see why Dorothy St. John had described her as the girl next door. She had a full head of curly brown hair and a pretty round face with delicate features that were becoming to her. I was embarrassed at the question that I knew I needed to ask.

Rodriguez could sense my hesitation and jumped in. She introduced us and told her how sorry we were about her roommate and what she had to go through when she came home to find her.

Arielle whispered, "Thank you," and seemed to be on the verge of crying.

Rodriguez was patient and gentle with her. She explained that we understood how difficult this was for her but that we needed her help to find out who did this to Nina.

Arielle nodded and Rodriguez continued, "Tell us about how you know Nina." The young woman related that they had met as freshmen at Niles West High School while trying out for the field hockey team and played together all four years and became close friends even though Nina went on to Wisconsin and Arielle to Drake University in Iowa. They remained close and saw each other during school breaks and a few visits in Madison. After graduating, they both had come home and were unsure about what to do next. Arielle said that she thought about giving modeling a try and contacted a few of the agencies. Ford was the first one to show interest and invited her to come in for an interview and to take some pictures. She asked Nina if she wanted to go with her and on a whim she did. They went to Ford, talked to Dorothy St. John and some of the account managers and they were both signed that day.

After a couple of months living at home and commuting into the city, they decided to get an apartment together and found their place on Illinois Street in River North.

"We love it there, at least we did," she said sadly.

"That's a pretty fancy address, Arielle, the modeling business must be pretty good."

"Oh, it is," she responded unconvincingly.

I decided to press her. "Arielle, we talked to Dorothy over at Ford she said that you and Nina worked the kind of gigs for her that might not be able to pay for that kind of building."

"Well, our parents helped us quite a bit."

"Your parents are well-off, Arielle? We talked to Nina's parents."

Arielle's face turned paler than it already was and her eyes dropped away from us to her knees.

Elaina took over. "We are not here to judge you or Nina. We are not looking to do anything here except find out who did this to Nina and the other young women found murdered in hotels in the same neighborhood."

"Do you think they are related?" Arielle asked looking wide-eyed and more alert.

"We aren't sure but we think it is very possible. You can help us to put some of the pieces together. Will you help us?"

Letting her emotions go, she began sobbing and said, "This is so terrible. We were just doing it for a while," Arielle whispered, "until we got the modeling going. We felt like it would be safe since we could watch out for each other. It wasn't supposed to work this way. We were supposed to be at home together or at least nearby. When I was leaving for the weekend to visit family in Ohio, I was surprised to hear her on the phone with someone, it sounded like she was making a date. I said, 'are you sure you want to do this while I'm away?' She just laughed, 'Don't worry, I got references. He sounds like a nice guy.'

"I didn't have time to argue or get more information. I just said, 'Let me know how it goes,' and left. When I didn't hear from her, I was a little worried but I thought maybe the date turned into a whole weekend, it happens and the money is really good."

I was hoping for some clue about who she was going to meet. We would do the usual phone search of her calls and texts but there is nothing like direct knowledge.

Unfortunately, she didn't have any idea. I took a flyer and asked, "Do you know a guy named Richard Kotler?"

There was a long pause. "How do you know about him?" she asked in a surprised tone.

Apparently, she hadn't been paying much attention to the local news.

I explained to her that Kotler had been acquainted with one of the other young victims.

She exclaimed, "Yeah, I know him. In fact, he wanted to see me last weekend, but the family trip kind of came up at the last minute and so I canceled."

"What can you tell us about him?" Elaina asked.

"I have seen him a couple of times," she replied, "he comes to Chicago often for work and likes the young ladies."

"Is there anything odd or unusual about him?"

"Well, he has a thing about neckties. He likes to use whatever tie he is wearing that day during sex. The first time he wanted to tie my hands behind my back and I said no. Then he wanted to choke me with the tie until I passed out; that was also a no go.

"He settled for me wearing his tie in a normal way."

"And nothing else, of course, other than that?" Elaina asked. "There was nothing creepy or kinky about him? How did you first meet him?"

"He saw me on the A-list and called. He gave me a couple of references and they checked out so I accepted the date."

"How does that reference system work out?"

"So far so good," she said, "most of the other escorts will give you an honest opinion about a guy. Mostly we want to know if they are clean and safe, polite and do they pay?"

"Do you know of any clients that Nina had a problem with?" I asked.

"We meet some real characters, but we stay on a price level that generally eliminates a lot of weirdos."

"What about a boyfriend?" I asked. "Do either of you have a steady boyfriend or have you been seeing anyone lately."

"We really don't have much time for that," Arielle said, "no one serious. We meet lots of people in this neighborhood and at modeling events but neither of us have had any steady boyfriends or problems with anybody. We have dated some but we mostly end up either on a job or with clients or working out at the gym. Most of the guys we see are fairly well-to-do middle-aged gentlemen. I can't think of anyone that either of us has dealt with that would do something like this."

"Okay," I said.

I gave her my card. "Please give us a call if you think of anything else or if you are contacted by someone that you are uncomfortable with. And one more thing, do you think Nina knew Richard Kotler?"

Arielle didn't hesitate. "Yeah, she was aware that I had dated him." "Would it have been out of bounds for her to accept a date with him?"

"No," Arielle replied, "between us, it's all business. If he wanted to see her it would have been okay with me, but I think she would have mentioned it."

We said our goodbyes and she thanked us, adding, "Please get this bastard."

"We fully intend to," I said.

Soon we were out on the sidewalk walking to our car. When we were a few feet away I noticed something that caused my senses to go on high alert. Traffic was moving along at a fairly brisk pace on Harrison Street except for a white SUV that was behind us slowing down to a crawl for no apparent reason heading east. In a flash I recognized the driver. I only had a split second to react. I grabbed Rodriguez and pulled her down behind a parked yellow van and yelled, "Stay down!" Then a barrage of automatic weapon fire poured down onto the van sending glass and metal shards flying all around and on top of us. The car was stopped in the middle of the street as pedestrians scattered. Traffic stopped in both directions. Another round of automatic fire rang out, further pulverizing the van. This time we both returned fire. The shooter was in the backseat on driver's side and I concentrated fire in his direction while Rodriguez fired at the driver. The shooter fell back into the car and out of sight. The driver managed to accelerate and drive off with a shattered windshield and side mirror. As they sped away, I got off a couple more shots that smashed through the rear windshield of the white SUV.

Elaina was already calling it in and put out an all-points bulletin out on the SUV which should not be hard to identify. We got into of our car and made a

U-turn with lights flashing and siren blasting. We were hoping to see them stopped on the side of the road somewhere but they had a good head start on us.

The debris from their vehicle only left a trail for about 1/4 of a block before fading away. There was no sign of them. They could have fled in so many different directions.

We started seeing squad cars flood the area. "You okay?" she asked me.

I looked myself over for the first time since the shooting had started. "Yeah, are you okay?"

She nodded.

All I could think was wow, neither one of us had a fucking scratch on us but that was way too close. This has got to stop. Who the hell are these guys? We then drove straight to the station which was buzzing inside and out. The shooting had gotten immediate attention from the media and the TV stations were rushing to get it on the midday news.

We brushed through the reporters and made our way inside. It was busier and more frenetic than usual. I noticed Captain Corcoran coming out of Lieutenant Whitehead's office looking grim. He didn't even look at us. We went into the task force room and everyone was there. Most of the detectives came over to us to ask how we were doing except Koz who sat at his desk. Not one of them was eating lunch or even drinking coffee which was not the norm for that time of day. Everyone seemed on edge. Simpson stopped talking into his phone and put it down on his desk.

Whitehead was coming in for a personal report on our investigation. Rodriguez and I only had a minute to sit down and check our messages. We each had one in particular that got our attention. Richard Kotler's attorney Laura Kopecky had left a message for Elaina and I had one from our mystery tipster. Before we had a chance to return the calls, Lieutenant Whitehead walked into the room. He wanted to know what Sgt. Simpson had to report and what we had learned from the autopsies. It was confirmed that the first victim had been drugged and then smothered probably with a pillow. The second was strangled manually indicating a powerful killer. The third died from the ice pick to the eye which went into her brain. She had a high level of alcohol in her blood. The autopsy on the latest victim had not been completed.

The killings didn't fit the typical profile of a serial killer since the manner of death had been either somewhat or vastly different in each case. It was now clear that each of the young women was working as an escort. We hadn't discounted the fact that all of the murders may not be related, especially the last one which was committed at a private residence rather than a high-end hotel and the murder itself was incredibly brutal and cruel. It was also hard to ignore the potential religious symbolism of this taking place on Good Friday of Easter weekend and the fact that Nina Eisen was Jewish.

Whitehead reiterated how much pressure was coming down on Chicago PD from the media and the mayor's office. He ordered us to work every day until further notice.

All overtime will not be questioned; it is expected. He wrapped up the meeting and told me and Rodriguez to meet him in his office right now.

We got up and followed Whitehead into his office. He motioned for us to sit down and he closed the door behind us. He sat at his desk and his demeanor softened.

"Are you two okay?"

We nodded yes.

"What the hell happened?"

I gave him a synopsis of our morning meeting and the shooting. I replayed the events and said that I was pretty sure that the shooter was Lucius Perkins a.k.a. L Train currently out on bail from the mugging incident.

Just then Whitehead got a call and listened for a minute and said, "Okay, thanks." And hung up.

He looked at me and said, "You're right, they just found Perkins dead in the backseat of a stolen white SUV in Jackson Park. He had a bullet in his left shoulder and his throat was cut from ear to ear. This thing has gotten out of hand. I am not going to take you off the street. We need all hands on deck for the escort murders case but I am going to order that you get some added protection in your home district. Don't object," he said when he saw us both looking uncomfortable. "This is not special treatment.

Whatever or whoever is coming after you two it doesn't matter. It's a real threat to you both and the public. This isn't about a mugging anymore. It makes sense and it could help us catch these jagoffs."

Chapter 8

Elaina punched in the numbers for Attorney Laura Kopecky and put the call on speaker. After first getting a receptionist. We were put through to Kopecky.

Elaina told her that she was on speaker with me.

She said that was okay. She was worried that her client hadn't shown up for a scheduled meeting at her office that morning and that he had not been to work or contacted anyone there. She called his cell several times but got only voicemail; texts were not answered. He had told her that he was going to Chicago for the weekend so she wanted to let us know the situation since we were anxious to speak with him. She wanted to wait another day before she filed a formal missing person report.

Elaina told her that we would make a few calls and asked her to let us know if he turned up.

We hung up with Kopecky and made some calls, put patrol on alert and checked some of the downtown hospitals but there was no sign of Richard Kotler. We decided to use one of the interview rooms again to call our mystery tipster.

This time I put in the numbers and hit the speaker of the desk phone. Soon we heard a familiar deep voice.

I said, "This is Detective Jack Fallon returning your call. We have Detective Elaina Rodriguez with us on speaker. May I ask your name?"

"For now you can call me Franco," he said.

"Okay," I agreed.

We will work on that later, I thought.

Franco continued. "I talked to one of the Austrians, the one I know best, Sophie, on Friday. She understood my concerns about their safety and thanked me but said that they were all very careful and she didn't like the idea of talking to the police."

"Understandable," I said.

"But this morning after the news hit about the girl on Illinois Street, she had a change of heart. She called me and sounded shaken. It seems that their group had apartments in that same building up until about a year ago.

"She doesn't know the poor girl but now she feels it could be one of them next. She has given me the go-ahead to provide you with her phone number but only if you give me your word that anything she tells you is off the record and strictly to be used to find the guy responsible for these murders."

"Franco, I'm going to switch off the speaker for a moment, I need to talk to my partner."

I looked at Rodriguez and she shrugged with a quizzical look on her face.

"I think we should do this," I said, "these women may know something. They might even know the killer without being aware of it. We use confidential informants all the time. We will need to keep this to ourselves, at least for now."

Rodriguez agreed.

I hit the speaker button. "Franco, are you there?"

"Yeah, I'm here."

"We can give you and the Austrians our guarantee that whatever we learn from you will be confidential except for the specific purpose of catching this killer."

Franco said, "Okay, man, I'm trusting you on this."

He was very firm that she would meet only with one male detective.

"It seems she is more comfortable with men, go figure," he chuckled.

He gave me the phone number and said he would tell her that Detective Fallon would be calling her.

I decided to give Franco some time to get in touch with the Austrians so we went back to checking out tips that were still coming in strong. After doing that for a couple of hours, Clyde Simpson came to our desks and said, "Lieutenant Whitehead wants us in his office right away. He wants you both to meet up with Youngblood and Skinner. He is worried about where that mugger case has been heading and wants to make sure that case gets full attention. But you are still working here. The escort murders are still top priority."

After the meeting with Lieutenant Whitehead Rodriguez gave Detective Larry Skinner a call. She knew him from the Police Academy and he grew up in Bridgeport on the South Side not far from Pilsen. *Another White Sox fan*, I thought. We agreed to go to meet with them at the detective station on West Belmont Street. On the way she asked me if I knew Detective John Youngblood very well.

I said that I did. "He was friendly with my previous partner Vernon Johnson. They were both veterans in their early 40s. They were from different parts of the city with Johnson being from West Side Austin District and Youngblood being from the far South Side Morgan Park neighborhood. They were both tough, street savvy, old school guys. He had been working gang task force for years and had taken Skinner under his wing. I had some minor dealings with Larry Skinner, enough to know that he was a few years older than me and played football at De La Salle High. He seemed to be a pretty good guy to me."

Elaina confirmed that he was cool and fearless on the job. It didn't take us long to get to the Belmont Station. We parked in the lot and checked in at the front desk. I knew the desk sergeant, a grumpy veteran named Kenny Huckabone. He was somewhere around 50, balding, a bit overweight and liked to chomp on an unlit cigar, whenever the white shirts weren't around. He saw us coming and took the cigar out of his mouth.

"Hey, Fallon, long time no see. I've been watching you do your act on tv lately. Glad you been busy. Is this the little lady that saved your ass?"

I laughed and said, "It sure is, Kenny, this is my new partner, Elaina Rodriguez."

I turned to her. "Elaina, this is Sergeant Kenny Huckabone, truly one of Chicago's finest. Don't worry, he's not as dumb as he sounds."

"Cut the crap, Fallon," Kenny growled.

He held out his hand to Elaina. "You're always welcome here," he told her, "much better looking than Johnson."

"Okay," I said, "that's enough of that. Where are you keeping Youngblood and Skinner?"

"Room 202!" he barked, "don't trip going up the stairs."

We got to Room 202 without a problem, much to Kenny's disappointment. I knocked and we went in. John Youngblood stood up from his desk and came over to greet us. We shook hands and I introduced Elaina. He pulled up a couple of chairs and we sat near their desks.

Larry Skinner said it was good to see me, it'd been a while and it was nice to know that I had Elaina for a partner. They exchanged a few pleasantries and then we got down to business.

Youngblood said, "I'm glad to see that you are both okay but I'm afraid this is not over. We have info from South Side gang detectives that have informants on the street. All three of the muggers were in a newly formed splinter group loosely affiliated with the Gangster Disciples. They call themselves the OP players, it stands for Ogden Park in Englewood. They have a psycho reputation and have been sending recruits up to Streeterville and River North to do muggings as an initiation. They steal cars from the South Side, come north on Lakeshore Drive, jump a couple of random people and head back south and dump the cars there. They turn over the loot to an older dude named Victor Melious a.k.a. Melo, age 25, with a long rap sheet, including violent felonies. He is anything but mellow. We have identified the mugger that got away from you in Millennium Park. He is 18-year-old Benji Jones, a.k.a. BJ from Englewood. He dropped out at 16 and has no known address. The word is that these punks have some backing from the GD's but they haven't quite earned their spurs. The South Side sources don't think they will stop coming after you. It is kind of a do or die situation and they want you to do the dying. We've got some pictures of BJ and Melo out to the patrol." He handed us paper photos of each one.

I recognized BJ immediately. He had short cropped jet-black hair, medium dark complexion and round facial features. He had angry dark eyes and something I hadn't noticed before. He had a one-inch scar just below his left ear. I did not recognize Melo. He clearly looked older and had medium length dreads, dyed with blond streaks with light milk chocolate colored skin. He was described as 6 foot, 180 pounds.

"We know that you guys are wrapped up in the escort case, we just wanted to let you know what we have and we are going to be expecting the possibility of more mugging attempts and more attempts on taking you two out. Our paths may cross and we will be there for you if you need us."

Skinner chimed in, "We've got your back, go get the freak killing these girls." We both got up and sincerely thanked them.

We all said we'd be in touch and we walked out. I gave Huckabone the finger as we left the building and Elaina winked at him which made his day.

On the way back to the station I decided to call the number for Sophie. We listened to some classical music before the call went to voicemail.

"Hello my dear, please leave me a message, I will return your kind call as soon as possible. In the meantime I will be thinking of you."

Rodriguez laughed out loud and I had to smile myself. "This is going to be very interesting," she said still laughing.

"I'll let you know," I said.

What am I getting into? I thought.

Back at the task force we checked messages and talked with the detectives that came in and out. Everyone had leads to follow but nothing clearly pointing to a specific suspect other than Richard Kotler and we were trying to track him down as well as we could without a missing person report being filed.

At 6:15 I decided to head home to have something to eat and relax for a few hours or so. I thought Elaina was going to stay for a while along with Zileen Baker and Morgan Latner. We were all working a lot of hours and were on call 24/7. We decided that it was a good idea for some of the task force to get some sleep early.

Outside the weather was turning milder and there was a soft southerly breeze.

You never know what you will get in April in Chicago but the temperature near 60 felt balmy. The drive home on Lake Shore Drive was pleasant with window down, and the calm lake with a slight roll of top water landing onto the shore. I allowed myself to enjoy the moment.

At home I took off my shoes and coat put my Beretta on the coffee table and laid down on the couch.

I had just started to relax into a daydream of walking on a sunny beach with no thoughts about work when my cell phone snapped me out of it. I answered it and heard a now familiar voice. "Hello my dear, this is Sophie. I am happy to return your call."

"Oh yeah, thanks," I said. "I'm hoping to meet you sometime soon."

"That would be lovely," she said sweetly. "I am very busy these days but I am able to see you this evening at nine if you wish."

I was taken aback a little. I wasn't expecting such an immediate response. "Sure," I responded. "Where would you like to meet me?" I asked.

"You may come to my apartment at Marina Village. It should be quiet here most of the evening."

I said that was fine.

She gave me the building and apartment number and the security procedure.

I had a couple of hours so I made a turkey sandwich and resumed my daydreaming until around 8:30, when I put my coat back on drove down to Marina Village and turned into the parking entrance of the East building and used the code Sophie had given me to gain entry. I drove up the winding parking ramps until I found the space she told me I could use. I parked, found the elevator and went up to the 35th floor. I knocked at Apartment 3502. The door was slowly opened by a petite, yet curvy, stunningly beautiful young woman with shoulder length light brown hair and penetrating dark brown eyes.

"Please come in."

She motioned me into a circular hall. I followed her into a living room with a crescent shaped blue leather couch, some multicolored chairs and a glass and steel coffee table. She invited me to sit down on the couch and she sat down breathtakingly close to me.

Despite the remarkable view of the Chicago River and sparkling lights from the buildings which form the beginning of the Loop, Chicago's supercharged financial center, I hardly noticed it. I couldn't keep my eyes off of Sophie in a revealing lavender dress which seemed to be straining to contain her curvaceous body in all directions. I struggled to focus on her face but her rich full lips and beckoning eyes made concentrating nearly impossible. Just then a buxom blonde woman in her mid-20s dressed only in a t-shirt and shorts walked into the living room. Sophie introduced her as Hannah.

She apologized for interrupting and asked Sophie if she could borrow some earrings. Her accent was more pronounced than Sophie's and they spoke in German for a while before saying it was nice to meet me. It was a pleasure watching her walk out of the room.

Sophie turned her attention to me and moved closer. My hormones which were already on high alert went to code red. She apologized for speaking in German to Hannah. She explained that they often switch between English and German without even realizing it. She said that Hannah and Mia had plans for the evening and would be going out soon. We would have the place to ourselves. She explained that they were six friends that shared two apartments at the Marina Village. She, Hannah and Mia primarily live there and Johanna, Valentina and Victoria mainly lived in the other, but that they are very flexible.

Sometimes they stay at each other's apartments. She explained that they all have busy schedules with full-time jobs or school and a very busy social life.

I was calming down a little and starting to think a little more like a detective. "Tell me more about the work you all do."

She smiled and I started losing my concentration again.

"I have an antique store in the West Loop which I run with Hannah, so we often travel to Europe and New York to buy items for our stores. Mia is a graduate student at the Illinois Institute of Technology in Chemical Engineering so she is in Chicago most of the time. Johanna sings at the Chicago Metropolitan Opera and travels quite a bit.

"Valentina is the oldest of our group and is very busy working as a personal trainer. She travels to Las Vegas and fitness shows but is usually in Chicago. Victoria works for a major real estate developer in the Loop and is usually here also."

"That is very impressive," I said honestly, "can you tell me more about what you call your social lives? You understand that the only reason I am asking about this is to see if you can help us catch whoever is killing young women like yourselves."

She leaned in even closer to me so that I could feel her breath on my face. "Yes, my dear, Franco told me why you are here and that we may trust you, is this correct?"

I had all I could do to keep myself from kissing her. I reluctantly pulled my head back out of kissing range.

"Yes," I said momentarily remembering what I was saying. Yes, to…"

I recovered enough to assure her that the police were only interested in finding the escort killer. She nodded.

Mia, a slender twenty-something young woman with coiffed auburn hair and hazel eyes came into the room to let Sophie know that they were leaving for the evening and would be home late. They were dressed to kill in form fitting dresses, high heels and light jackets. Sophie said something to them in German, they smiled and waved to me and were off into the night.

"Let's have some wine," Sophie said, and went to a wine fridge in the room and pulled out a bottle of Austrian white wine. She poured some wine into two Austrian crystal pear shaped glasses and handed one to me before sitting back down on the couch. Any closer and she would have been on my lap. She put her glass forward and we clinked glasses as she said, "Proust."

I said, "Cheers."

We took a drink, she put her glass down on the table and leaned in again, practically whispering. "We normally do not tell anyone about our social business. We are a society of friends, all from the University of Vienna. We are 30 women living in Wien or Vienna, as you say in English, New York, Chicago, and Las Vegas. Those of us in the U.S. are all here legally and we all have jobs or go to school full-time. We are brought together by a desire to provide the highest sensual pleasure in the most enjoyable and professional way. We make friends and meet new friends only through referrals from our other friends, so you see, we value our privacy and our friends' privacy. This is why I first told Franco no when he asked me to speak to you but this morning when the news came out about the poor girl found on Illinois Street, we became even more frightened than before. You see, we lived in that building before we moved here about a year ago."

She took another drink of wine and I joined her.

"We go to these same hotels to visit friends but we also visit them here. One of the reasons we left that building was because there were problems with the security there."

"What kind of problems?" I asked.

"People were coming into the building through doors in the back with no security. They were supposed to be locked but they were often left open. There were a couple of apartments broken into. We didn't feel safe."

"I'd say you made the right call there."

"Yes," she whispered, moving even closer, "we need to be smart; we try to look after each other. I feel very safe right now," she said, slipping her arm to my shoulder.

Now I was the one feeling nervous. I was getting almost too excited to get my words out.

"I have to ask you one more question!" I exclaimed. She frowned, almost pouted.

"Okay, I'll let you ask me one more question."

"Do you have a friend named Richard Kotler?"

She paused and said, "He is not one of my friends, but I think he is known to Johanna and Valentina. Now I have a question for you," she whispered into my ear; as she slipped her leg across my lap, I could clearly see that she was not wearing underwear.

I had thrown in the towel.

"Do you want to be my special friend?"

She now had her other hand on my inner thigh. "I don't know, I don't think I can afford it."

She began kissing me on the neck while whispering, "With my special friend, there is no money."

She moved in to kiss my lips and moved her hand to my crotch. I enthusiastically reciprocated and began caressing her perfectly rounded firm breasts. I moved my hand down to begin stroking her groin; she was moaning a little and breathing hard speaking in German. She undid my belt and pulled my zipper down with her left hand. Soon she was kneeling in front of me and licking and sucking my balls, she then moved up to do the same to my throbbing cock. Her mouth was moist and warm, and her tongue caressed me into an explosive orgasm. I shook with pleasure and she didn't lift her head until she had swallowed the last drop. When she finished, she looked at me and said, "that is the best drink." She proceeded to take all of my clothes off and led me into her bedroom. She placed me down on her king-size bed on my back and her dress came off in an instant. She straddled me and leaned over to kiss me deeply. I could see her perfect breasts with subtle brown nipples lightly bouncing up and down. I moved both hands from her breasts to her perfectly proportioned firm behind. I was hard again right away and she hopped on me in one easy move and began rhythmically swaying slowly back and forth and moving up and down. I caressed her breasts and she spit some saliva on herself and I rubbed it into her firm tits. She began moaning again and saying something in German. I don't know what she was saying but it turned me on incredibly. She was so wet and hot I had to hold onto her hips and try to wait for her to reach her climax, and after a few more wonderfully erotic minutes, we both came at the same time. We continued to kiss gently until she rolled off to my side and continued to caress me.

She whispered sweet words in my ear and began kissing it and placing her tongue inside my ear, making a warm moist erotic sensation. Before long I was fully excited again and went down on her to lick and taste her sweet clit and pussy. She squealed with delight and started exploding with multiple orgasms. I moved off and placed my cock in her moist, torrid, dripping pussy; our bodies moved in sync and her moaning became louder and almost sounded as if she was crying in joy. She was still exclaiming some things in German and then began shouting it. It took me longer to come this time and she seemed to be coming continuously. When I finally did come, she moaned and said, "Oh my God!"

A couple of hours later I woke to find us stuck in each other's arms. She began stroking me and kissing me warmly. I couldn't resist. We made love again and it was just as erotic and sensual as it was earlier.

Afterward, I realized that I needed to go. She accompanied me to the living room where I dressed and got ready to leave. She stood before me in all her naked beauty and kissed me. She said, "You are now my very special friend, please call me again."

I thanked her and said that I would. I wasn't really so sure about that but I knew that it would certainly be tempting. "Let me know if anything comes up that you think I should know," I said when leaving.

"I will be happy to," she replied.

I walked out the door leaving behind an incredible visual by which to remember her.

Chapter 9

The morning came too soon on this Tuesday. I was tired and moving slowly. The shower woke me up a little and I drank a cup of vanilla hazelnut coffee from my single cup Keurig with a slice of wheat toast. The day was partly sunny and mild around 58° with a light breeze from the west. I hit Lakeshore Drive and found heavy traffic heading downtown. I was still tired but feeling a mellow satisfaction from my time with Sophie last evening.

I wasn't sure how I would handle it with Elaina. I had crossed the line with a potential witness, and I didn't want to drag my new partner down with me if this somehow came out. I decided that discretion was the best way to go, it may not have been valorous, but it was safer for myself and for Elaina.

I got to the station at 8 a.m. and beat Rodriguez for the first time. About half the group was there and everyone was on the phone or computer and it seemed clear that nothing dramatic had happened overnight. Elaina came in a few minutes later and I told her that I had gotten my call from the Austrians and had gone to Marina Village for a meeting with Sophie. I relayed the basic picture of their little society that Sophie had painted for me the night before. I mentioned that they had lived at the building on Illinois Street and had found the security to be lax. I said that I think we should check that out this morning and Elaina agreed. I also relayed that a couple of the Austrians may have interacted with Richard Kotler and that we should probably see if they would talk to us. "Sounds like she was very cooperative," she said with a raised eyebrow and a sly smile.

"Not that cooperative," I chuckled, "I think we should give Kotler's lawyer a call," I said changing the subject.

I used our desk phone and dialed Laura Kopecky's number and hit speaker. The call went through reception and soon I had Attorney Kopecky on the line. I informed her that Detective Rodriguez was with me.

She said, "Good morning to you both." She then said that she was starting to get more worried about her client, he had always been very responsive to her calls in the past.

"We would love to help you out," I said, "but as you know, we can't go put a trace on his credit cards unless someone files a missing person on him."

She said that that was understood, she wanted to talk to one of his partners first, and she would get back to us later that day.

Outside at the car we assumed our positions in a white Chevy Impala sedan. On the way I called the building on Illinois Street and was eventually put in touch with the manager. A pleasant-sounding woman named Natalie Watts whom I guessed to be somewhere in her 40s.

I explained that we were close by and she said that she would meet us near the front door. When we arrived, she met us, and we noticed a doorman sitting behind a desk to our right.

She said that she expected we were there about Nina Eisen. We nodded.

She noted that she had already spoken to detectives Simpson and Stone but that she would help in any way she could. She explained that there was a doorman on 24-7 and that residents were contacted before anyone was let on to the elevators. The parking garage required a code just to get in and then there was an attendant. "What about in the back?" I asked.

Natalie explained that there were a couple of service doors that were kept locked and either she or maintenance would open them for deliveries.

I asked if we could walk outside and around the building to the back and she grabbed a jacket from behind the desk.

We walked out to the street, the air was still mild and the sun was playing peekaboo with the passing clouds. We walked to an alley and turned up it and then left to the back of the apartment building. I could see two doors. We went to the first one and pulled on it, but it was a strong metal door and locked tight. The second door looked the same but opened right up when I tried it. Natalie's look turned from confidence to dismay.

"I don't know how this is possible!" she exclaimed sounding exasperated. "We have strict rules about this since we had some complaints last year about uninvited people getting in and now with everything going on, I can't believe it. I need to talk to maintenance. Please come with me to my office, we have our security set up there."

We went into the building and she locked the door behind us. We passed a stairway. I could see only one camera and it was pointed away from the stairway. I walked over to the stairs and looked inside and did not see a camera. "No cameras in the stairway?" I questioned.

She looked down and shook her head. "No."

We stepped into the elevator and I could see the camera there.

"Were the cameras in the building working this past weekend?" Elaina asked.

"Yes and no," Natalie said, "I'll show you in my office."

We got to her office and she invited us to sit down in front of the security monitors. She typed in something into her phone and said, "I've sent a message to Fred Zerlo, the head of maintenance to come to my office."

She logged into the security system and it went to Friday night.

"I knew you would want to see this," she said, "I've already shown it to the other two detectives."

We watched the lobby video footage for a while without seeing anyone that looked like our guy. We switched to the elevators without noting anything suspicious, then the door opened and a figure in a mask, knit hat, gloves and raincoat stepped in, lifted his arm, and sprayed the camera without looking at it. It went dark. The elevator went to the 15th floor and the monitor switched to the camera in the hallway. The mystery man kept his head down and went right to it and walked past. He then reached up to it from the side and all you could see was the arm and the black gloved hand and then it went dark. It looked like our guy around six feet tall with dark hair, Caucasian, and average build. We stayed and watched for hours of frustrating footage through that Friday night into Saturday morning. Our suspect was never seen there again. We figured that the intruder could have left on the stairs and gone out the same way he came in. A camera in the back alley had been sprayed like the others.

I called Simpson and told him what we were doing, and I explained that I had some info that the building had a soft spot in the security and that it had checked out.

He said that he and Stone had viewed hours of the CCTV and that included nearby buildings on Illinois Street without coming up with anything.

I told him that that we were probably covering the same ground and I would stop that for now and wait to talk to the maintenance guy, Fred Zerlo.

Fred finally showed up after finishing cleaning one of the vacant apartments. He was a big imposing man around 50. He seemed a little uncomfortable looking at the expression on Natalie's face. Fred was informed that Natalie had been showing us how secure their building was and was made to look pretty damn foolish when we got to the service door. Fred looked down at his well-worn work boots. "Even after all that has gone on here, you leave the damn door unlocked?" his boss said scowling at him.

"I…" he stammered, "I had a delivery coming and I didn't want to get bothered while I was fixing the appliances on the eighth floor. I know I screwed up."

"Can we ask you a couple of questions?" I said.

He nodded sheepishly.

"Did you leave the back door unlocked Friday?"

"I don't know, I don't think so…" he stammered again. "I might have," he admitted.

"How late did you work on Friday?" Elaina inquired.

"I came in at 7:00 and left at 4:30 Friday. After that I was on call, you know standby on Saturday, and my assistant Dominic was on call Sunday. We both had Easter Sunday day off."

"Did you see anything unusual Friday?" I asked.

"No," he replied, "we had a few deliveries, but they were all familiar people who were in and out. I may have left the door unlocked over the weekend for any Saturday deliveries." He seemed like he might cry. "I feel terrible about this, it's just that we've always done it this way."

I said, "Old habits I guess."

"Then I did it again today, yeah old habits I guess."

"I will deal with this later," Natalie said curtly. The look on her face even made me a bit uneasy.

My partner and I made our way out into the mild early afternoon. I was starving and suggested we swing over to the nearby Harry Carey's for lunch. I had a friend from high school that worked there, and I hadn't seen her in a while. We found a parking spot on West Kinzie and walked through the covered sidewalk entrance and through the front doors of Harry's. We went in and to the right and then into the long bar area to the left. We found a couple of seats at the bar and sat down. A cute brown eyed bartender with long jet-black hair came over to us smiling broadly.

"Hi there, Jack, where the hell have you been?"

"Kinda busy," I said with a grin.

"I know, I've seen your name all over the news."

"I'm trying to cut back," I quipped. "Lisa, this is my partner, Elaina Rodriguez. Elaina, this is Lisa Pastore. Lisa and I went to Fenwick together. She was a star lacrosse player."

Lisa chimed in, "That was only because they wouldn't let me play football." Elaina and I laughed. Lisa is about five foot two and 100 pounds.

I ordered a Holy Cow Burger, medium, with crispy bacon and Gouda cheese. Elaina decided on the roasted turkey club on their whole-grain bread. Lisa walked the order into the kitchen and later came back to chat some more.

"You seem to know a lot of cute bartenders," Elaina said.

"Well, those are my favorite kind," I replied, "do you two have a history?"

"No, I always kind of had a crush on her but we were usually dating other people.

"On a more serious note, have you told your husband about how serious this threat is from the mugging case? He must've seen the shooting on the news."

Elaina kind of sat back and said, "Actually he didn't see it. We don't watch the news at home, and I haven't wanted to frighten him or the kids."

"I get that, but I think your husband should know to be aware, that's all. Just consider it. It's pretty clear that these guys have no ground rules. They know no boundaries."

"I'll think about it," she said.

We enjoyed our lunch and I had a chance to catch up a little with Lisa. She had a little boy now which I knew but I couldn't believe that he was already in kindergarten.

She asked about Gina and said she was sorry to hear that we weren't still together. She said that she always liked her and thought we made a good couple.

"We did. I just am not ready for the house, the kids, and the forever part of it."

"How about some dessert?" she asked.

"No thanks, Lisa, I wish I could. You have the best tiramisu in the city. I'll stop by another time when I can stay for a while."

"Okay, you do that; nice meeting you, Elaina. Take care of this guy."

"I'll do my best," Elaina said.

We were out the door and soon back at the station. We were briefed on the findings of the autopsy done by the ME on Nina Eisen. It turned out she had no drugs and only a small amount of alcohol in her system. She had bruises on her throat and there were other indications that she had been knocked unconscious but that was not the cause of her death, what killed her was she simply bled to death. It was a slow, cruel way to die that took many hours, possibly more than a day. As with the others there was no indication of a rape and sperm or other bodily fluids found on the body. The crime scene investigators could find nothing that would lead to a suspect. The only usable finger prints were those of Nina and her roommate Ariel Katzenberg. And the fact that the blood samples were all from the victim frustrated the detectives that had been trying to find any common threads connecting all the victims. There was absolutely nothing other than the fact that they were all young, attractive escorts. That kept bringing us back to Richard Kotler or someone like him.

I decided to call our tipster Franco to try to get something more from him. Elaina was busy following new leads that had come in that morning. I called Franco from my desk phone and soon I heard his deep gravelly voice say, "Yeah?"

I started by thanking him for the introduction to the Austrians. Then I told him about my meeting with Sophie, leaving out the more personal and steamy aspects. I asked him if he had heard anything from Kotler or the mystery man that had introduced him to the Austrians.

He said, "Not in a while, nothing from Kotler and nothing from his friend who had come back to Chicago sometime in March after an extended business trip to Europe."

I told him that I understood that he did not want to identify his friend, but I just wanted enough info to possibly eliminate him as a suspect.

He said, "What do you have in mind?"

"Can you give me a general description of him?" I asked, "just his height, weight, and age bracket."

He was silent, then he said, "Yeah, I could do that. He is around six feet, 190 pounds and he's around my age."

"What about his hair color?" I asked.

Franco laughed. "He keeps it dark if you know what I mean," he chuckled.

Unfortunately, this did not eliminate the mystery man. I had asked Sophie to describe Franco, and what she told me did not eliminate him either; around six feet tall, 200 pounds in his 50s with brown hair.

I thanked him again and asked him to let us know if he heard from either one of them.

He said he would do that.

Next, it was time to get back in touch with Laura Kopecky. When I got through to Attorney Kopecky, she seemed upset. "My client's business partners are very reluctant to file the missing person report. They seem to be wary of what may come from this. They are a very conservative bunch. Personally, I would have filed by now, but they want to wait another day."

"Okay, let's keep in touch."

"Will do," she said.

Elaina and I continued to follow up on the leads that were still coming in. We had the late desk duty, so as the rest of the team started filing out, we were the only task force members left by 6 p.m. We ordered some Chinese food from China Wing Doll on North Wells Street and settled in for more phone and computer work. At around 7:30 I got a call from Detective Youngblood, and he asked where I was. When I told him, he asked if Rodriguez was with me. He then asked me to put her on speaker so that she could hear.

Once I did, he asked if we both could hear his voice. We answered in the affirmative.

He began in a serious tone. "We have just received some credible information from the South Side gang unit that there is something big brewing out of Englewood. The informant told the detectives down there that he thinks these new gangster wannabes, the OP players have gone off the deep end trying to prove themselves to the GD's and that they were planning to take out two detectives from the Near North and that they didn't care how they did it. I think you know which two detectives they are talking about."

"We do, John," I said, "do you have any info on what they are planning?"

"He said only that it's expected to happen very soon. I think we have to be ready for just about anything. We will be in constant contact with the gang unit and we are going to be keeping an eye out around your station and your homes. We are taking this extremely seriously and you should too."

"Thanks, John," I said, "we appreciate what you and Larry are doing." Larry Skinner then spoke directly to us.

"Hi, Elaina, don't take this lightly; you too, Jack. I know you two don't scare easily but be especially cautious. We will keep you informed of anything new. Watch your backsides."

We hung up and Elaina and I just looked at each other. The worry on her face was obvious. "I need to call home," she said urgently. She was driven by an overwhelming desire to protect her children and husband. They decided that Paco and the girls Rosie and Lucy would go to stay with his brother's family in Cicero for a few days. She would join them this evening after work.

I didn't have the same sense of urgency myself. I wasn't going anywhere. It wasn't that I didn't think it was serious, it was I just wasn't going to let these assholes drive me out of my home. We settled back to work on the leads but nothing much panned out. No news on Richard Kotler or anything else. At one point Elaina hung up the phone call she was on and looked at me.

"Why did they do it? Why do escorts do it? Do you think it is right?" she asked.

"I really never gave it much thought until a few days ago. I guess they do it for the money."

"Sure, of course," she said, "but I don't understand why a woman would do that."

"Well, I think some women actually enjoy it," I said with a laugh.

Elaina didn't think it was funny. "I would never want that for my daughters."

"I understand completely," I said, "but I don't think it should be illegal for consenting adults. The whole issue of people being forced into it is a completely different thing to me. I really think that women should be able to do it if they want to."

Then, foolishly, I added with a laugh, "With your looks you could do it."

That really seemed to hit a nerve. She started speaking rapidly in Spanish and I was pretty sure that she wasn't agreeing with me.

"Okay, okay, just joking. Let's focus on what we have in front of us. I think we have enough to worry about right now."

She got calmer and said, "You're right. Whether or not these women should be doing it, we need to stop this monster."

The rest of our shift passed on unremarkably. We called it quits around eleven and headed to the parking lot. We checked all around us and looked under our cars and under the hood. Nobody was around. It was another mild night, unusual for Chicago in April but we welcomed the forecast that called for more of the same for another day or more. Hallelujah! While driving home I couldn't help looking at every nearby car or pedestrian suspiciously. I kept thinking about my former partner, the veteran Vernon Johnson who liked to say, "Always be aware of everything around you, never take anything for granted."

Chapter 10

I woke up Wednesday morning with an uncharacteristic feeling of anxiety. My job had always been somewhat stressful and dangerous, but I rarely let it get to me. This was one of those times. I felt like I was waiting for the other shoe to drop on both of these recent cases. As I readied myself for my workday, I didn't have my normal desire for a quick run or even any breakfast. I just wanted to get on the job.

I dressed in a lightweight dark tan suit anticipating another mild April day. While driving Lakeshore Drive, I got a call from my dad asking me how I was doing. I said that I was fine and everything was good.

He expressed that he had been worrying about me but didn't want to call and get me worried about him.

"Something has come up from one of my attorneys at the public defender's office," he said, "he has been representing a young kid from Englewood on pretty serious armed robbery charges. The kid is looking for a way out and yesterday he contacted our office saying he needed to see his lawyer right away. She went to Cook County jail and he said that he had direct information regarding a plan to kill some cops. She arranged a quick meeting with the State's attorney's office and they offered him a deal. It hasn't been formalized yet but I am jumping the gun a little bit by calling you now. We are bound by confidentiality but there is an exception to prevent a future crime that could result in serious injury or death."

"Thanks, Dad," I said, "to be honest I have been on edge a little today, my partner and I were informed yesterday by the detectives that took over the mugging case, that there is word on the street that some guys from that wannabe gang in Englewood are coming after us hard and soon, but no specifics."

"You are right to be on the edge," Dad said, "our information is a bit more specific. According to our client the hits are being carried out by the mugger

85

that got away from you, Benji Jones and the reputed leader of the OP players. Victor Melious known as Melo. And here's the scariest part, they're going to use bombs."

"We have been aware of that possibility, Dad, but this is something new." "That's right," my dad said somberly, "Chicago street gangs have rarely used bombings in recent decades."

I told him that Elaina had moved last night to her brother-in-law's home in Cicero. I also asked him, not to share that info with anyone. I knew that I could trust him on that.

He offered his house to me but I appreciatively declined. I would never want to put him or my brother and sister at risk and I am just stubborn enough to want to stay hidden in my own apartment.

My dad ended the conversation by asking me to take care of myself and telling me that he loved me.

"I love you too, Dad, thanks for everything else." We hung up.

While I thought this day was already getting intense, at the station everyone was going about their business. There were no new developments overnight again. I told Elaina that we needed to use a conference room for a call. Once there I relayed the gist of my father's phone call.

I told her that I was going to call the office at my apartment building and warn them about accepting any packages or envelopes and to watch the mailboxes.

"How are things at your brother-in-law's?" I asked.

"It's fine," she replied, "for a few days anyway. It is a little crowded, but the girls think they are on vacation."

"Okay, I don't think you should go near your house for a while. Once the State's Attorney's office formalizes the deal with the informant, I'm sure we will be called in and told about all this. I promised my dad that I wouldn't tell anyone about our conversation. I'm sure he understands that I would have to tell you."

"Understood," she said.

I called the office at the Covington Apartments told the building Manager Trudy Lane about the potential threat and that she may be getting a call or visit by detectives or patrol officers later that morning. I wanted her to know about it right away.

She seemed a bit shaken and even though I had only known her for a couple of months, she sounded sincerely worried about my safety.

I thanked her and told her that I felt terrible that they could be in danger at the Covington, and she said that she would inform the doorman immediately.

"Okay, do what you have to do."

Elaina called her husband and her next-door neighbor in Pilsen and gave them the warning. "Be suspicious of everything and don't touch any packages or envelopes."

We went back to the task force room and didn't have long to wait before we were called in to see the Lieutenant.

Whitehead asked us to sit down and told us about the deal just made with the informer in the State's Attorney's office. The Lieutenant was worried for our safety and the escalating nature of this threat. He said we were welcome to go on desk duty or even take a paid leave of absence.

"We both would rather not," we said in unison.

"We are better off on the street. We can do more good out there," I said.

"Okay," Whitehead reluctantly agreed, "I am placing a uniform on your personal cars and we will not be accepting any packages or normal mail delivery for as long as it takes. There is already a citywide bolo for Benji Jones and Victor Melious."

"Thanks, Lieutenant," we said. And then we were out the door.

We returned to our desks and decided to call Laura Kopecky again. Richard Kotler's attorney was soon on the line with me while Elaina took another call.

Kopecky said she was just about to call me. "No one had heard from Kotler and his partners, were now ready to act. They were going to file a missing person's report with the Milwaukee PD and ask them to coordinate with Chicago since they have reason to believe he may be there and we're going to release the information. I asked if he had any business credit cards that she knew of. She said that the partners had cancelled them."

"Okay, that's good news. Do you know if your client had access to a significant amount of cash?" I asked.

"Yeah, his office told me that one of the reasons they have become more alarmed is that $10,000 in petty cash is gone from the company safe and no one signed for it. And only the partners had access to it."

"Okay," I said, "we will probably be talking again soon."

The missing person's report had been in effect for only about an hour before it produced some results.

A call came in on a possible sighting of Richard Kotler at the Talbot, a hip boutique hotel in the Near North on Delaware Place. Kotler had sort of become our suspect within the task force so Sgt. Simpson told Elaina and me to get on it now.

We hustled out to our car which was under guard by a patrol officer and after a quick inspection, we raced the short distance to the Talbot with lights flashing. We stopped in front, told the doorman we needed to leave it there and ran into the sleek black and gray lobby and to the front desk.

We didn't have time to find out who called the tip in, we just needed to know whether Richard Kotler was still there.

The young woman at the desk took a look at our stares and seemed to grasp the urgency of the situation. She started in on her computer and after about 20 seconds she looked up and my heart sank.

"I'm sorry, detectives," she said meekly, "Mr. Kotler checked out this morning, just 30 minutes ago."

Damn, I thought, *it was just 11 o'clock and we missed him by 1/2 an hour.*

"Damn, how long was he here?" I asked.

She went back on her computer. "He had stayed two nights used the bar one night and the restaurant for dinner both nights but paid for everything in cash. He did register a credit card but since it was never used the card info was cleared when he checked out."

We were directed to the bar and found a bartender and a server getting ready for lunch. We showed each of them a picture of Kotler and got a response from the server. She remembered serving him dinner on Monday night. He dined alone and she didn't remember anyone even talking to him.

The bartender had been off Monday and Tuesday.

Well, it was clear that he had been there but he didn't seem to have made much of an impression.

I thought that we should drive around the immediate neighborhood to see if we could spot him. Elaina agreed and drove first toward the Lake and Oak Street Beach. The mild weather brought walkers, bikers, and runners to the lakefront path.

We got across Lake Shore Drive and drove along the beach road and didn't really see anyone matching Kotler's description.

We drove back across the drive into the Gold Coast area and drove through the well-heeled streets of million-dollar townhouses, boutiques, and slick restaurants and bars.

We walked into some stores and restaurants, hoping to get lucky but by 12:30 we felt like we were wasting our time and that we could cover more ground from our desks.

We didn't have the time or inclination to eat in the Gold Coast so we picked up some sandwiches at a 7-Eleven and went back to the station.

We barely got started on our lunch when a call came in about an assault that just took place on a young woman at an apartment on Superior Street in River North. 911 took the call from a hysterical young woman who said she thought that the Escort Killer just tried to murder her.

Because of the reference to the Escort Killer, 911 referred the call to our task force. Most of the detectives were out so Sergeant Simpson gave it to us.

We put the sandwiches down and went back to our car which was still under guard. We jumped in and drove off. We got to the building just west of State Street on Superior. There were a couple of squad cars already there and one of the patrolmen took us up to the fifth floor and into a modest one-bedroom apartment. Sierra Montero, a young attractive woman in her early 20s was sitting on the living room couch dressed in jeans and a very flattering, pink t-shirt. She was visibly shaken and had a noticeable bruise on her forehead and bruise marks on both arms. Her breathing was heavy, close to hyperventilating.

Elaina sat next to her and said something in Spanish and placed her hand on her arm that seemed to calm Ms. Montero down.

She switched back to English and asked the young lady to tell us what happened.

"I invited a friend over today to hang out for a while. Everything was fine. We had a couple of beers and were listening to music when all of a sudden, he attacked me right here. He grabbed me and we struggled. I kept pushing him off and he hit me in the head. I blocked it but he was too strong, it still got me right here." She pointed to the bruise on her forehead which also had started to swell slightly.

She excitedly relayed that she thought he was going to kill her and was only saved because the doorbell rang. "It was a delivery. It spooked the guy and he got up and ran out the door."

"Okay, Sierra, what does this guy look like?"

"He was a white guy about 5'10" with light brown hair and about 30 years old."

We looked at each other.

"What was your friend's name?" I asked.

She seemed to get nervous. "His name is Mike."

I looked at her until she said, "I just met him recently. I don't know his last name."

"What made you tell 911 that the Escort Killer tried to kill you?"

Sienna now was uncomfortable. She said, "Did I say that?"

"Yeah, you did."

"Well, I have to tell you something, I don't want to get into my any trouble. I am going to school at City College and I work part-time. I can barely afford this apartment after Brent, my roommate, moved out."

"Okay, we understand," I said in a quiet soothing voice, "we are not worried about charging you with anything. We're only after whoever is targeting young women like yourself."

"I decided to try escorting," she blurted out, "I was nervous about it but I put an ad on the A-list. This was my first time and I swear it will be my last." She started sobbing.

Elaina put her arm around her and asked, "How did he contact you?"

"He replied to my online ad by email. I was an idiot. I didn't have his last name or a phone number or anything."

"Did he give you any references?" I asked.

She looked puzzled. "I didn't even think of that," she replied mournfully.

While we were certainly interested in running this guy down, we knew that he wasn't our guy. Almost everything about this guy didn't fit but he needed to be off the street.

We thanked Sierra Montero and told her that some patrol officers would finish the interview.

We went back to the station and reported to Sergeant Simpson. It was a serious case but it was not our guy. We went back to our desks and spent a few more hours tracking new leads and calling four- and five-star hotels hoping to hear that Richard Kotler was staying at one of them. No such luck.

Elaina and I told each other to be safe and Elaina headed to her car for the ride to Cicero and I headed to Uptown. Somehow it didn't seem possible that it was only Wednesday. The unusually warm weather normally would be a boost to my spirits but I hardly even noticed it on the way home.

I pulled into my parking space at the Covington Apartments and tried to notice everything around me. I was looking for the littlest thing that might be out of place or anything that didn't seem right. I had never been so apprehensive in my life.

Up in my apartment I kicked off my shoes, took off my jacket and holster and popped open a Miller. I sat in my recliner put my legs up and stared out my living room windows, enjoying the view toward the park and the Lake.

I turned on Sirius XM and put it on 90s hits and tried to chill out. A couple of hot dogs and a couple more Millers later, I was beginning to feel nearly normal.

At around 7:30 my phone lit up. I could see that it was Sophie. I was very tempted to ignore her call but something told me to answer. I was glad that I did.

She was frantic. Her cool professional demeanor was replaced by the sound of a frightened young woman.

"I am so very worried about Valentina and Mia. I got home tonight and they were gone. They went with him. They could be killed, Jack. I need you to help them. Please, Jack, please."

"Wait a minute, wait a minute," I said, "slowdown, Sophie. Why do you think they are in trouble?"

"Because they went with that man you are looking for, Richard Kotler. We try to keep track of each other when we go to meet our friends. We are not usually worried at all but we only have each other to look after us. When I got home Johanna was here and she told me that Valentina and Mia had gone out to meet a guy who wanted Valentina to bring a young one with her so they went to meet him at the W Lakeshore Hotel at 7. They were aware that you were looking for Richard Kotler. But Valentina had met with him before and she wasn't worried. I am worried, Jack. I would have talked them out of meeting him. Can you help them? Please hurry."

"Thanks, Sophie. I am on my way."

My sense of calm was gone in an instant. I put on my shoes, jacket and gun and I was out the door. At that time of night on a Wednesday in April, the traffic was moderate. It would only take me about ten minutes to get to the W Lakeshore at the corner of inner Lakeshore Drive and Ontario Street. It is a four-star hotel with half of its rooms looking out to Lake Michigan, Ohio Street Beach, and Navy Pier. I called Elaina and told her what was happening and asked her to call for a patrol car to stand by but to approach without lights.

I arrived at around 8 I pulled into their semicircle driveway and parked to one side. I identified myself to the attendant outside and showed my star. I walked briskly into the lobby and to the bar area. I did not see Richard Kotler or the Austrians. I decided to go to the bar instead of the front desk. Bartenders usually notice everything and I knew that Kotler liked to have a drink with his dates.

There were two bartenders on and the first one to greet me was a young man named Nigel. I pulled up Kotler's picture on my phone and showed it to him.

"Have you seen this guy in here tonight with two young women?"

"Bingo," he said, "you just missed them by about ten minutes. They all had a drink and then walked out the main door where you came in."

Dammit, I thought.

"Are you sure it was this guy?" I asked, showing him the photo on my phone again.

"Yeah, I'm sure. He was with two hot women. One was taller and a little bit older than the other, shorter and younger, but they both were striking."

I said, "Thanks," and hurried to the exit.

Outside, I showed Kotler's picture to the guys doing the valet parking and manning the doors.

They said they had seen him leave a little while ago. He was with two hot chicks.

They walked south on Lakeshore toward Ohio Street.

My mind was racing; where were they going? I saw a patrol car pull up and I went to the driver and asked him if he had seen a middle-aged guy with two attractive women? He had not.

I told him to stay there and to hold them if they came back.

I ran across Ontario, past a couple of cabs that were waiting for fares from the W.

There was no one in the cabs except the drivers, I ran past them onto the corner of Ohio Street and Lakeshore. Now I had a decision to make. They could have gotten into a cab and now could be anywhere. They could have walked straight toward Grand and the entrances to Navy Pier but I didn't think that was likely. They could have walked west on Ohio Street. There was nothing on the first couple of blocks of Ohio except office buildings and apartments.

It was still mild and there was only a soft breeze from the south. I decided it could be the beach. I ran to the stairway leading down to a tunnel that goes under Lakeshore Drive leading to Olive Park and Ohio Street Beach. There was no one in the tunnel until just before it ended. A couple of runners came into the tunnel from the park and blew past me. I have to admit they caught me off guard and I almost pulled my Beretta. I ran up the ragged stairs into the beginning of multiple pathways. One going Olive Park which is thick with trees and bushes and dark. There's another pathway going north along the Lake which was lightly populated with runners, walkers, and bicycles. There was a young woman at the far end of the beach playing with her black lab which didn't seem to have any problem with how cold Lake Michigan is in April.

I decided to talk to the woman with the dog to see if she had seen anything.

I walked to the shoreline to get to firmer sand and I immediately was stopped in my tracks. A cloud had moved past, revealing some moonlight onto the water in front of me. On top of the water gently rolling to the sand was a motionless body of a young female about five feet out face down in the water. I ran into the Lake and cautiously rolled her over in the knee-deep water. I feared the worst and I was right; the woman's eyes were wide open and lifeless. I picked her up out of the water, keeping her head steady in case of a head or neck injury even though I was fairly certain that she was gone. I was still clinging to the slightest hope. I placed her down on the soft sand and called 911. I started doing CPR, hoping to hear or see some sign of life. She was gone and I knew it but I kept trying until the ambulance showed up. I turned her over to the EMTs. By that time, the woman and black lab were gone, and I didn't see any likely witnesses.

I decided to ignore my soaked shoes, socks, and pant legs and walked back to the W to see what they had on the closed-circuit TV. When I got there, I asked the guys out front if they had seen Kotler come back and they had not. I went to the front desk and asked when Richard Kotler had checked in.

The young woman said, "I'm sorry, Detective, but we do not have a Richard Kotler registered here, there is no one named Kotler."

"Could he have checked in with cash without showing ID or a credit card?" I asked.

"Absolutely not," she said with authority.

I smiled and said, "I didn't think so, just had to ask. Who do I talk to about taking a look at your video?"

She said, "That would be security. I will ask someone to talk to you right away." Soon a well-dressed, powerfully built guy in his mid-30s came out from the elevators and introduced himself as Leon Culpepper, Assistant Head of Security.

I did the same and explained to him what happened and asked to see the footage from the entrance lobby and bar from 6:30 to 7:30.

He said he would check with the control room and make sure it was set up for me.

Just then Elaina came flying into the lobby. Culpepper walked off and I relayed to Elaina what happened and brought her up to speed.

Culpepper came back and I introduced him to Elaina. He led us to a small but well-equipped video room and asked us to look at one of the screens. He started with the lobby and we didn't have to wait long before Richard Kotler came into view. He was wearing a black two-piece suit with a white shirt and a black and red striped tie. He came in and went directly to the bar and ordered a mixed drink. About 15 minutes later Kotler took a call on his cell and ten seconds later the Austrians walked over to him. The taller one with dark brown hair, blue eyes, and an athletic build, gave Kotler a courtesy kiss on the cheek and introduced her companion, an attractive young woman with auburn hair and hazel eyes. I will never forget those eyes. It was Mia, the poor soul that I found floating in the Lake. The taller woman I recognized as Valentina.

They sat down on either side of Kotler and they both ordered what looked like some kind of a martini. They leisurely sipped their drinks, chatted and the Austrians were friendly, leaning in to talk to him and touching him from time to time on the arm or the thigh. When they finished their drinks, the bartender came over to see if they needed another round. I could see Kotler looking at his companions and then say, "No."

He took the check and paid in cash. They got up and walked arm in arm out of the main door.

The outside camera showed that they walked out of the driveway and started to cross Ontario, going south toward the cabs and then we lost them.

There was no way at that time to tell where they went after that. We only knew that Mia ended up dead in Lake Michigan.

We left the video room and saw Leon Culpepper in the lobby. We thanked him and gave him a card asking him to call us if Kotler showed up.

"I think we need to go to Marina Village," I said.

Elaina agreed and we planned to drive over together. She would bring me back to get my car later. I cleared it with the door attendant and we left for Marina Village.

On the way I called Sophie and she still sounded frantic.

"Oh Jack, I am so worried. Valentina came back without Mia and she is so upset I can't get her to talk to me. What happened, do you know anything?"

"Sophie, I'm coming to see you with my partner. We will be there in a couple of minutes, hang on."

We parked inside the building with the code provided by Sophie. We were also able to take the elevator up to her apartment. She let us in and I introduced her to Elaina.

She was dressed in a sweatshirt and sweatpants without any makeup. She looked like a nervous wreck. She whispered to us that Valentina was in the living room with Hannah. She relayed that she had arrived home in a hysterical state and had barely been able to talk. "I took her damp sandy clothes off of her and put her in something warm. She has always been the most sensitive one of us," Sophie said.

"Sometimes little things can make her very upset and emotional. You see, her mother had a very serious mental illness and she lost her at an early age. Please be gentle with her."

I said that we would and Elaina nodded, then came the hardest question.

"Have you found Mia?" she asked, almost pleadingly.

I looked at her for what was surely only a couple of seconds but seemed like forever. "We are so sorry," I whispered.

Sophie almost fainted into my arms. "Oh no!" She sobbed. "Please no, Jack, no." I patted her head and then lifted her up and back standing under her own power. "Tell me now, Jack. I don't want Valentina to hear anything bad right now."

I told her that we found Mia in the water off Ohio Street Beach. She was already gone. I said, "We don't have all the answers yet, but we're going to have to ask Valentina some questions."

"Okay, I will bring you to her," Sophie said.

We followed Sophie into the living room and found Valentina basically in a fetal position on the couch and Hannah sitting next to her with one arm around her. They were also dressed in sweatpants and sweatshirts and heavy socks. Valentina had her face buried in her hands. Sophie directed us into chairs across from Valentina and then sat next to her. She patted her on the shoulder and said that some nice detectives are here to help us, we need to talk to them. She then said something to her in German and Valentina looked up at us. She looked almost childlike, both bewildered and frightened.

I let Elaina take the lead, I figured Valentina's feelings toward men might be a bit negative at that moment.

"Valentina, my name is Detective Elaina Rodriguez. I know that you are upset. This may be very difficult, but we have to ask you some questions. Can you help us?"

Valentina sat up a little straighter and nodded.

"Can you tell us what happened tonight from the beginning?"

"Tell them in English Valentina."

"Yes. Earlier today, I got a call from Richard, a guy I have known and met with before. He wanted me to meet with him at the W Hotel by the Lake. I said okay. I never had any trouble with him before. He was clean and polite and generous. This time though he wanted me to bring another girl. He had never asked for that before but it was a normal thing for some guys. I said I would check and let him know.

"He said okay, but he wanted a young one so he could have one old and one young. I felt a little bad, I do not think I am so old, so I asked Mia if she would like to join me with him? She said she was free, so why not?

"I called Richard back and told him okay. He asked if we could meet him at the bar at the W at 7."

"We are talking about Richard Kotler, right?" I asked.

She responded, "Okay, yes, it was Richard Kotler. We knew that he dressed formally and the W is a nice hotel so we put on some pretty dresses and were looking good for him. When we got to the hotel he was already at the bar. We called him first and he said to come in and we sat with him and he ordered a drink for us. Everything was very normal. He said that he wasn't staying at the W and would like to take us to dinner before going to his hotel."

"Did he say where he was staying?" I asked.

"No, he didn't say. When we got out, we were going for a cab on the corner, when he said it is so nice out let's take a little walk on the beach first. It was early and it was his time so we said okay. We walked down to the tunnel that goes under the street and went to the beach. Mia and I took our shoes off, the high heels don't work in the sand."

Valentina smiled for the first time, just for a split second. "We walked across the beach to the water and walked along it going toward the park. We were just chatting about how nice it was, nothing really, then out of nowhere, he turned on Mia and started swearing, kind of growling. He put his hand around her throat and said that he was going to kill her. He called her terrible names and said that he was going to kill her first and then me.

"I jumped on his back and tried to choke him. I told Mia to run and she did. He was too strong for me and he threw me off and down on the sand. I thought he was going to kill me, but he ran after Mia. It looked like she would get away from him so I ran in the other direction and went off the beach and up into the park. I ran all the way to Navy Pier and then stopped to look behind me. I was so scared. He wasn't there. I didn't even realize that I had held onto my shoes and purse. I was happy to at least have my purse and wallet. I walked west on Grand Avenue until I was able to get a cab to come home. I could barely tell the driver where I lived. When I got here, I had a meltdown but I will be okay now. You need to find Mia; she must be out there trying to get home. I don't know if she still has her purse."

I looked at Sophie as if to ask with my eyes do you want me to tell her? She tightened her lips and nodded. She put her hand on Valentina's arm.

"We found her at the beach," I began, "she was in the water. She didn't make it."

Valentina began shaking. She went back into a full fetal position with her head in her hands. She was crying loudly and violently.

"This is all my fault, this is all my fault. I never should have asked her to come with me."

I stood up and Elaina followed.

"We are very sorry for your loss. Thank you for seeing us, we will be in touch and we will let ourselves out."

Sophie just nodded and she and Hannah were covering Valentina like a blanket.

Elaina drove us back to the W to retrieve my car. The mild April night belied the storm that was brewing.

Chapter 11

I was having trouble sleeping again and woke up early on Thursday morning, around 5. I got up, shaved and showered and ate some cereal. I had a cup of coffee and it was still only around 5:45. I decided to go to Montrose Beach to see the sunrise, not having grown up near the lake I had never done that. The parking lot at the beach was dark and empty and cold. I had taken a look at the weather before leaving my apartment and the temperature had plummeted overnight. I was happy to have worn my overcoat. It was still dark when I got to the beach but there was a slight shimmer of light far off into the horizon, and soon there was a pink ribbon stretching low across the sky. The whipping wind was chilling me to the bone and made my eyes water and my nose run, but I was transfixed to the crown of gold emerging as if rising out of this vast inland ocean. It was a wonderment to me that here I was in the middle of this dynamic raging juggernaut of a city all alone at one of the city's major beaches, watching nature's daily miracle all by myself. I felt like shouting at the top of my lungs, do you all know about this, why are you not here, but selfishly I was happy for the solitary experience. I watched until the golden orb was fully out of the water shining its life onto me in the great city of Chicago.

I went back to my car and cranked up the heat. I got to work by seven and was the first detective in the task force room. At that time the Cook County medical examiner's office was just about to open so I called hoping to have some answers concerning Mia's cause of death. My call was routed to Dr. Lacey Gorman. I had worked with her before and knew her to be very thorough and competent.

She greeted me with, "Oh, good morning, Detective Fallon, glad you called. I was just finishing my overnight shift. I think I know what you are calling about. Mia Bauer."

"Right, yeah," I replied, "the young woman brought in from Ohio Street Beach last night. Did you work on her, Doctor?"

"Yes, I performed the autopsy. The Lake didn't kill her, Jack. She didn't drown. There was no water in her lungs. Her neck was broken, literally snapped in one twist. There were no other injuries or indications of ongoing abuse. She was otherwise very healthy, no drugs, not even a trace and a small amount of alcohol. She hadn't been in the water long before she was brought out of Lake Michigan. So we have a broken neck as cause of death and homicide as a manner of death. The formal report will be out later today. Right now I need to go home and get some sleep."

"Okay, Doctor, one more thing. Did you find anything on her when she was brought in?"

"She wasn't wearing too much, Jack, not even any underpants. It was a little odd though, she was only wearing one shoe."

"Okay, thanks again, Doctor."

I sat back in my chair and realized that with everything going on last night, I did not notice or at least remember anything about her feet or shoes.

The task force detectives started coming in. I was glad to have missed the morning news. TV crews apparently had gathered outside the station after I arrived. Koz seemed particularly perturbed by their presence and somehow blamed it on me. He was strutting around the room waving his arms. "They're all out there looking for our big hero. They're asking for you, Fallon. Why don't you go out there and take a bow?"

I stood up and said, "Why don't you go out there and kiss your own ass?"

He turned red and started to come toward me. Sergeant Simpson walked in between us and told us to sit down and shut the fuck up. Koz sat back down, partly because Simpson outranked him but mostly because he would have mopped the floor with him.

He turned to me, "You too, Fallon, sit down." Order was restored.

Simpson announced that there would be a team meeting as soon as everyone got there. A few minutes later Elaina came into the task force room and sat down next to me. She looked tired.

"Everything okay?" I asked.

"Yeah okay, but not great. My brother-in-law's house isn't big enough for all of us and my kids have gotten sick. They are crying to go home, so not a lot of sleep. We'll get through it. How about you?"

"I haven't been sleeping too well either," I replied. "It did cause me to get up and go see the sunrise though, I wasn't sleeping anyway. It was really awesome. Nice way to start the day. Anyhow, I called the ME and caught Dr. Gorman before she left. She did the autopsy on Mia Bauer. She said that her neck was snapped in one sharp twist, no water in her lungs, no drugs in her system."

Dios mio Elaina whispered while crossing herself, "Poor girl, I think we should call Kotler's lawyer."

I picked up the desk phone and was happy to hear the receptionist say that she would see if Attorney Kopecky was in and again was pleased to hear a voice say, "This is Kopecky."

I asked her if she had heard anything from her client?

She replied that she hadn't. She also didn't know anything about what happened at Ohio Street Beach last night. Apparently, Milwaukee has their own problems.

I related the events of last night and that we had some reason to believe that her client committed the murder of Mia Bauer and possibly several others. We would love to have him turn himself in.

"I understand," Kopecky said, "I will talk to him about that if I get the chance. I was going to call you this morning anyway. There is something going on at Kotler's company. Things have seemed strange in the way they have been reluctant to get the police involved and haven't seemed very forthcoming with me. I'm going to tell you something if it can be off the record."

I said, "It could be if what you have to tell me is not directly related to crimes committed in Chicago or where I can find him."

Kopecky said her information was related to neither of those things. "It may not even be related to my client," she said, "but I think you should know that Kotler's firm has discovered that they have a lot of money missing and I mean a lot of money, in the millions. One of our secretaries has a friend who works at Kotler's company in their accounting office. They have had an audit going for a few months now, and things are coming to a head. There is a huge amount of money unaccounted for and only two of the partners had the ability to have diverted this kind of money to personal accounts.

"They have not gone to the local authorities at this time. They probably don't want it to get out. They may be hoping to recover the money without any publicity. Only one of the partners is in the wind, and that is Richard Kotler."

I could hear Sergeant Simpson's voice telling us to wrap up what we were doing. I thanked Kopecky for the information and hung up. Simpson gave everyone a minute to finish phone calls or whatever else they were doing and then started the meeting.

"Okay, listen up everyone. I think you are all aware by now of what happened last night at Ohio Street Beach. We have another victim and she fits the profile of the other escort murders and she was known to be with one of the persons of interest immediately before her death. This can be corroborated by several witnesses and we have a witness that claims to have been another intended victim and to have seen our suspect Richard Kotler, a businessman from Milwaukee and frequent flyer in the escort world, attack the victim on the beach before she escaped and ran into Olive Park, leaving Richard Kotler and Mia Bauer still on the beach. Fallon and Rodriguez have been looking at this guy Kotler for a while and have cultivated some contacts in the case. One of the contacts paid off last night with a tip about Kotler having a date with two escorts. They are victim 24-year-old Mia Bauer, a student at IIT and Valentina Bruner, a fitness instructor and personal trainer at one of Chicago's top fitness clubs downtown. They are both Austrian Nationals in the Country legally. So, right now this investigation has gotten even hotter and more focused. We are going to put a full court press on to find Richard Kotler. Detective Stone and I will work on writing up warrants for the arrest of Kotler as well as pinging his phone and monitoring his credit cards and bank accounts. I want detectives Baker and Kozlowski to concentrate on the airports.

"Start with O'Hare and Midway but contact the smaller airports in Cook, Dupage, Kane and Lake Counties as well. Latner and Sanchez, you take the train stations and bus depots and run down any vehicles Kotler may have rented or that he has registered in his name. Del Signore and Schmidt will stay based at the task force central for now, taking the leads that come in and calling hotels near O'Hare and other areas of North Side. Fallon and Rodriguez will follow up on the most recent murder and concentrate on hotels in River North and Streeterville. Detective Fallon, you were on the scene last night and have been on this Kotler character from the beginning, do you have anything to add?"

"Thanks, Sergeant," I said as I stood up. "Rodriguez and I have had Kotler as a strong person of interest because he fits the general description of our suspect and because he has had a known relationship with one of the previous victims, Janelle Park, and is known to frequently employ escorts on his regular trips to Chicago. Just this morning I have learned that there could be something else going on which could affect Kotler's behavior. He may be on the run in connection with a very large sum of money that has come up missing from his company in Milwaukee. If this is true, he may be running off the rails. This guy may have started out as a serial killer and now be on a spree. We don't have any knowledge that he possesses any firearms but he is physically strong and should be considered very dangerous." I sat back down.

"Okay, and are there any questions?" Simpson asked. "You all have your assignments."

"Let's go get this guy," Elaina said, telling me that she wanted to go to the Ohio Street Beach crime scene.

I said, "Ok. Let's put on our overcoats and hit the beach."

The area immediately surrounding Ohio Street Beach and the beach itself was cordoned off to the public. The crime scene investigators were still searching and sifting through the sand and surrounding area.

We parked on the inner drive and walked down into the tunnel onto the beach.

We found the officer in charge of the scene and walked on up to her. Neither Elaina or I were familiar with this crime scene investigator. Her name was Sergeant Camilla Flores. We introduced ourselves and stood near the water I was now feeling stiff and cold. The hawk was coming hard off the lake. The water was much rougher than it had been the night before. A couple of investigators in wetsuits were walking out of the rough water.

One of them was holding a woman's high heel shoe and handed it to Sergeant Flores. "It's the only thing we came up with, Sarge, not much out there at this time of the year." Flores took the shoe and put it into an evidence bag.

"The ME said that Mia Bauer was brought in to her wearing only one shoe," I said, "seems likely that they found her other shoe. I pulled her out right about here a few yards into the Lake." I told Elaina at the time I didn't even notice her feet. I was concentrating on trying to revive her and had to be very careful because of a possible head or neck injury. I didn't know that she was already dead from a broken neck.

We went over what Valentina had told us and decided to follow her trail. Walking first along the water and then up the beach past the restaurant building and up to Olive Park. We found the nearest path which wound its way through the small park and out onto Grand Avenue. We took our time and walked off the trail at times. We were thinking that Kotler, after dispatching Mia, may

103

have followed after Valentina, hoping to find her still in or near the park. We didn't find any signs of Valentina or Kotler. We went over to the main entrance of Navy Pier which was as far as Valentina got before turning around and heading west on Grand Avenue. We didn't think it would be fruitful to stay around the pier since there wasn't usually much of anything going on there at that time of year and it was unlikely that there was anyone around that would have seen anything from the previous night, but I still called in to ask for some uniforms to canvass the area anyway. Simpson called as we walked back through the park toward our car, and he said that a suspect had been picked up in connection with the assault on Sierra Montero. "Name is Chuckie Florentine from Jefferson Park, age 26, with long light brown hair." He was obviously not our guy. Someone was going to interview him.

Simpson wanted us to hit the Near North hotels next. There are roughly 64 four- and five-star hotels just in Streeterville alone. So we had our work cut out for us. We started with Grand Avenue and worked our way through the hotels on the main east-west streets in the neighborhood. Wherever possible, we would each take a hotel armed with our pictures of Richard Kotler. It was slow going. We tried to make sure that we checked with every doorman, concierge and front desk person at each hotel. By noon we had only covered 16 hotels.

We went to Epic Burger which was nearby on Ontario Street for a quick lunch.

After inhaling our burgers, we resumed our search through the privileged halls of some of Chicago's finest hotels. We covered a few more on Ontario, making our way to Michigan Avenue. I took the Intercontinental and Elaina took the next hotel on Michigan, walking north toward Erie Street. When I got to the front entrance of this grand old Chicago classic there was Uncle Don in his doorman's uniform that would be appropriate at a royal palace in Europe somewhere.

He greeted me with a big toothy smile and a pat on the back, "How are you, Jackie?"

"I'm doing fine, Uncle Don, we're all working hard to find this guy Richard Kotler." I showed him the picture on my phone. He said that he didn't recognize him but would keep an eye out. I told him that I would send him an email with his picture as I had been doing with other doormen and front desk agents. "I have to go in and talk to the front desk now," I said, and I told him, "Good to see you, Uncle Don."

"You too Jackie. Good luck."

"Thanks," I said and went into the impressive rotund lobby. I stopped by the front desk and the concierge and made sure that I sent a copy of Kotler's picture to either their phone or their computer. I waved to Uncle Don on the way out while he was hailing a cab for one of his guests. Elaina and I spent the rest of the afternoon visiting Streeterville's finest hotels without finding our man.

We did talk to several people who recognized Kotler from previous days but no one who had seen him recently. At around 5:30 I checked in with Sergeant Simpson and he said that nothing much had turned up at the airports, train stations or bus stations.

Latner had found a car that was registered in Illinois to Kotler. He also had owned a condo in the South Loop up until December and a bulletin had been put out for his silver Mercedes but it was unclear whether Kotler had been driving it in recent months. He said that he realized that Elaina and I had been working late the last couple of nights and told us to go home and get some sleep and hit it hard again tomorrow.

We went back to the station and checked our car in. We went to our own cars and found them still under guard. We got in and went our separate ways. I didn't feel like going straight home and I couldn't think of anything better than a few beers at my favorite place for ribs, the Twin Anchors in Old Town. It didn't take me long to get to this classic neighborhood tavern on North Sedgwick. I found a spot and parked about 1/2 a block away and walked through what was now a howling frigid wind out of the north to the small but legendary Chicago rib joint. I walked into the unassuming cash only rustic tavern and spotted an open seat at the bar and sat down. I ordered a bottle of St. Pauli Girl and a full slab of ribs with fries and their famous Spicy Prohibition sauce. They had the local news on one TV and ESPN on another. I chatted with the bartender, a guy named Mark that I had seen before, but didn't really know well until my ribs and another St. Pauli Girl showed up. It didn't take me long to polish them both off, just long enough to get through the sports and weather and a few commercials. I always have had a good appetite. Just as the last weather forecast ended, there was breaking news coming out of Pilsen. I felt a chill run through my body.

"Mark, do you mind turning the sound up on the news?" I asked.

He shrugged and said, "Okay."

There was a reporter on the scene standing in front of what looked to be a house that had experienced a bad fire, then the on-scene reporter with excited tones started her story.

"Tonight only 20 minutes ago, there was a massive explosion near the front of this home in Pilsen. As it happens, the residents of the home were not present but one of the neighbors, a woman named Maria Silvera was killed while collecting mail at the home for the residents who were away. We are not able to give you any further information at this time. We will have more on this story on news at nine."

My phone started buzzing.

It was Elaina, "Jack, thank God you are there." She was rambling on mixing English and Spanish.

I said, "Elaina, calm down, I'm okay. I didn't go straight home. I'm at a restaurant in Old Town, no problem here. I just saw the story from Pilsen on the news."

"That was our house, Jack, our fucking house, I feel responsible. My neighbor, my friend, Maria. Oh God no. She wanted to keep my mail for me, I told her not to." She seemed near tears. "I swear to God Jack, I told her not to do it."

"Elaina, I'm very sorry, are you all together in Cicero?"

She said that they were. I told her, "Don't go anywhere tonight."

"Jack, you shouldn't go home. Either stay with your dad or your brother or sister."

"I will figure something out," I told her.

I really wasn't sure what I was going to do but I didn't want her to have any more stress on her than she already did. I got a notification that another call was coming in.

"Elaina, it looks like Whitehead is trying to reach me, take care of yourself. Hold onto your kids and don't blame yourself."

I took Lieutenant Whitehead's call. "Hey, Lieutenant. Yeah, I saw the news from Pilsen. I just talked to Rodriguez. She's okay. She's in Cicero with her family."

"Where are you, Jack?"

I told him where I was and that I was good.

He said, "Don't go home tonight. I'm sending a bomb squad to your building and an extra patrol. I want you to stay there and figure out somewhere else to go. I want to have some backup, clear the area around Twin Anchors. Wait a half an hour."

I said I would. Might as well have one more St. Pauli's, I thought and ordered one from Mark. I felt in a quandary. I had resisted getting any of my family involved but I also had the Lieutenant telling me not to go home with good reason. I didn't want to walk into an ambush and I really wanted to keep my job. I was not going to get my dad involved. I knew that I already had enough to worry about without getting him directly involved. He had a lot of stress himself just with his job as First Assistant Public Defender in Chicago. My brother Barry has a wife and two small kids, he was out. That only left my sister Molly. She was up in Evanston and doesn't have any kids or even a husband to worry about. I gave her a call. She was home and was happy to have me stay with her even after I explained what had been going on and the risks involved. I felt guilty but I knew she wouldn't have it any other way. I wasn't surprised to learn that she wasn't aware of the bombing in Pilsen or even the escort murders that I had been working on. She enjoyed staying in her academic world and avoiding the harshness of Chicagoland's daily drumbeat of crimes and hardships. She didn't care about the Cubs or Bears whether they win or not or even if they play. If she wants to know what is going on with the weather, she would rather just look outside the window than turn on the television.

Sometimes I envy her serenity but I realize that I am hooked on the rush I get from dealing with the energy, challenge and danger that runs through the veins of this Goliath of a city. I told Molly that I would see her in about an hour since I was going to take side streets as much as possible to make sure that no one followed me to her apartment in Evanston.

I finished my beer and left my cash on the bar with the check. With my overcoat on and collar turned up. I walked out the door and down the one step and onto the sidewalk. I turned left to walk south on Sedgwick with a cold wind pushing me along. I was tense. I looked all around me and tried to notice everything as I traveled the half block to my car. I didn't see anyone or even any cars which made me nervous. I looked under both ends of my Camaro and saw nothing unusual. I got into the car and hesitated for a minute even though I knew no one could have of gotten under the hood without setting off the alarm. With a deep breath I started the engine and pulled out, driving north on Sedgewick with still not a soul around. My plan was to drive north for a while, going on to some side streets to make sure there was no one following before eventually cutting east over to Lakeshore Drive.

On the way to Evanston, I continued on Sedgwick encountering light traffic and nothing suspicious. I turned left on Armitage and noticed that a dark colored sedan followed me from Sedgewick. I went a few blocks and took a right on Cleveland. The sedan followed again. Now I was getting suspicious. The windows in the sedan were tinted, revealing two figures but not much more. At the first side street, I turned left and the sedan came with me. I looked back, but still could not make out the figures behind me. The unfamiliar streets were dimly lit and I slowed down. I saw a street sign coming up on the right and decided on one more turn and if the sedan followed, I would call for backup and confront them. I was monitoring the sedan as I turned onto the dark street and for a moment my Camaro was off the pavement and suspended in air. It landed with a thud at a 45° angle with the passenger side resting in the dirt of a completely dug up street. I quickly unhooked the shoulder belt and began extricating myself from the car. I needed to hold the car door open with one leg while pushing my body up and out.

I could hear female voices, "Hey, are you okay?"

I saw a hand holding the door which made it much easier for me to get out and into the dugout street. Next to me were two young women from the dark sedan that I thought had been following me. They were not turning, but stopped when they saw me take a nosedive. The girl that held the door for me said, "Wow, this is crazy."

I looked around. There were no signs, no construction barriers, nothing indicating that the road had been under construction.

They asked me if I needed them to call for help and I said no I could handle it.

They got into their car and pulled away, and as they did, I looked down the street and could see a Chicago PD patrol car heading toward me on the paved street which ran straight into my dug out one. I thought this is cool, maybe these guys can get me pulled out of here. The patrol car stopped about 20 yards from me, and two uniforms got out. They waved and went to the back of the car and opened the trunk. I was thinking that they must be getting shovels or something else to help me out. The trunk closed and they each began moving around the patrol car on different sides. My sense of relief suddenly turned to alarm. They were holding shotguns and their uniforms didn't fit.

Everything seemed to go into slow motion. At 10 yards I recognized them. It was BJ and Melo! At eight yards, BJ started to raise his shotgun. In an instant I dove back toward my car and into the 4-foot hole of the street. The shotgun blast passed over me, raking my car, but missing me entirely. The fucking dug up street had momentarily saved my life. I could hear them saying something, but it was unintelligible. I pulled my Beretta and tried desperately to think of a good strategy to fight back. I didn't have one. Suddenly, there was the screech of tires and doors slammed and a voice said, "Get back, Larry." I heard a shotgun blast, then a loud groan and gunshots from a revolver. I lifted up and started shooting. I hit the closest uniform to me, and I heard more shots ring out to my left. The second uniform went down too. In moments it went silent. Through the smoky hazy night, I could see three bodies on the ground and Detective John Youngblood kneeling over one of them. It was Detective Larry Skinner. He was holding his head up off the pavement and imploring him to hang in there.

He told me to call 911. He gently put Skinner's head down, took off his overcoat and placed it under the head of his gravely wounded partner. He then took off his jacket and used it to put over the gaping hole in Skinner's stomach and placed enough pressure there to stop the bleeding. He was stroking Skinner's head and calmly telling him he was going to be okay.

I instinctively went to check on the attackers. I went to BJ first and could see that one of my shots had caught him in the head. He had no pulse. Melo was hit in the chest and arm but was breathing. I kicked the shotgun away from him and took my coat off and followed Youngblood's lead and placed it under Melo's head and removed his gun belt. I took my jacket off and tried to stop his bleeding as well. I called 911 again to make sure they sent two ambulances.

In a few minutes they started arriving, one patrol car and then another, and they started setting up a perimeter and diverting whatever traffic came in our direction.

The first ambulance arrived, which Youngblood made sure came to Skinner first. The EMT's took over and quickly had Larry Skinner on a gurney and into the ambulance and started poking in IV's. Soon the second ambulance arrived and EMT's took over, treating Melo. Within ten minutes the ambulances were on their way and we were left standing in a crime scene surrounded by the smell of gun powder and flashing blue lights.

John Youngblood came over to me, he was visibly shaken. "That damn kid, I told him not to go charging out there. Damn, more guts than brains. We were trying to lay back from you while still having your back. We got held up on Armitage and we fell too far back."

"Jack, what the hell happened here?"

I told him about how I thought I was being tailed and didn't have any warning before turning into a dug-up street without any signs or warnings of construction. I had no idea how these jagoffs got a patrol car and uniforms.

"I'm afraid that this is going to get a lot worse," Youngblood said.

We soon learned just how right he was. Two detectives arrived on the scene and I recognized one of them but didn't really know either. They approached Youngblood and shook hands. He seemed familiar with them and I knew that there would be several rounds of interviews as a result of the shooting, especially a fatal shooting. There would be Homicide detectives, State's Attorney's, investigators, and Internal Affairs. These guys were Homicide but from a different district, and when they finished with Detective Youngblood, they came to me. Detectives Lewis and Xander made their introductions and took my statement and my Beretta.

They said that it appeared to be a good shoot, but they would get back to me.

Before leaving, Detective Lewis had some bad news. They informed us that earlier that night the bodies of two patrol officers, Ryan Dolan and Naomi Wilkes were found in an alley in Old Town, both stripped down and shot in the head. Dolan was 25 and on the job for four years and Wilkes was 23 and she was in her first year on the job. BJ and Melo were driving their patrol car.

My phone buzzed and it was Sergeant Simpson. "Jack, it's good to hear your voice."

"Yeah, it was really hairy, Sarge, if it wasn't for Skinner and Youngblood, you wouldn't be hearing it. Do you know where they took Skinner? I want to go to see him."

"I know how you feel, Jack, but that won't be necessary. Skinner was just pronounced at the hospital. I guess Melo is hanging on, but they aren't optimistic about him either. Damn, Jack, the bomb squad has cleared your building. I wouldn't let my guard down, but I think you can go home. We are hoping that this will be the end of the OP players. Come in early tomorrow, Jack, you're going to have more interviews and we still have our own murder cases to solve. You've got the Lieutenant to see tomorrow and other interviews."

I called Elaina and I could tell she hadn't been sleeping. She said that she was so happy to hear from me among other things in Spanish that sounded happy and angry at the same time. "Sergeant thinks it may be over, so I am going home," I told her.

She said that they were going to stay in Cicero for a while, since there was significant damage to the front of their home and would take a while to get it repaired.

Next, I called Molly, another person glad to hear my baritone voice. She had seen something on the news which she was watching because of me. She broke her routine because she was so worried. I appreciated her more than I was able to say and at that moment, I appreciated all of them for everything, and I was lucky to have them.

"Good night, Molly," I said.

"Good night, Jackie," she replied.

Chapter 12

The pounding rain woke me up from another short night of sleep. Everything seemed out of focus. The downpour blurred the views out of my windows and my state of mind seemed just as clouded. *Am I really remembering all of this right?* It was as if a couple of years of intense police work had been crammed into less than two weeks. It was only 6:00 a.m., but I knew that I had to snap myself out of it. It was going to be a long grueling day beginning with the interviews and meetings that needed to be endured setting the record straight about what had occurred the previous night. I went about my morning routine minus any sort of breakfast or even coffee. I simply had no appetite. The shower helped, especially the cold blast of water at the end. I put on a navy-blue suit, Oxford blue shirt and a navy tie with a maroon stripe and put on an overcoat.

When I got to the task force room Simpson came in and sat down next to me at Elaina's desk.

"Jack, I'm really sorry that this thing got so fucking out of control. What started out as a serious but seemingly simple mugging case, somehow ended up with seven people dead, including three officers."

"Did Melo go too?" I asked. Not that I really cared. Dolan, Wilkes and Skinner were still dead. And Melo was still a piece of shit.

"Yeah, he died in surgery early this morning. You will probably be put on desk duty at some point, but that order hasn't come down yet. Still, I want you and Rodriguez to man the phones and run-down tips for now. You will have some explaining to do with Internal Affairs and the State's Attorney's office, but I don't think there will be a problem."

He paused a moment to let that all sink in. Then has asked, "Did Homicide take your gun last night?"

I nodded yes.

"Lieutenant Whitehead wants to see you and Rodriguez as soon as she gets in. The Internal Affairs officers will be here at 9 a.m. and the State's Attorney's investigator at 10:00. In the meantime, let's not lose sight of what we are all doing here."

"I hear you, Sarge."

He got up and went to his desk as detectives started coming in. They all stopped by to at least say something positive, even Koz who just said he was glad we got the cock suckers. My basketball buddies, Latner and Del Signore shook my hand and sincerely expressed how happy they were that I was sitting there.

Elaina came in looking as tired as I felt. She sat down next to me and just said, "Jack, I feel so terrible about Larry Skinner."

I replied, "You were right about him. He was fearless. He saved my life. He took a shotgun blast that would have been me if he hadn't stepped in the line of fire. I don't know what else to say. He truly acted heroically."

She turned away and stared down intensely at her keyboard without making a sound.

I waited a couple of minutes and nudged her shoulder. "Whitehead wants to see us. Let's go."

I knocked on the Lieutenant's open door and he motioned us to come in and sit down.

"I wanted to see for myself how you two are doing," he said. "In all my years on patrol and as a detective, I have never seen anything like this. Gang members have never targeted the police in Chicago. I hope this is not the beginning of a trend. Thank God you both are okay. Jack, I understand you have meetings this morning with Internal Affairs and the State's Attorney's office. Elaina, I have scheduled an appointment for you with one of the Department's Psychologists. Jack, I want you to make an appointment in the next few days. You aren't officially on desk duty, but for now I'd like you to coordinate and support the other detectives from the station and take any tips that come in. There will be flags of mourning flying this week and there will be a formal police service for the officers we lost last night announced by the superintendent's office." Whitehead dismissed us and we went back to the task force room.

The morning was fairly uneventful for both of us until my meetings with Internal Affairs and the State's Attorney's office. A Representative began the meetings that were professional and cordial.

It seemed like Youngblood and I were likely looking at a justified use of force. Elaina said that the psychologist was okay, but she made her feel uncomfortable. I haven't met a cop yet who likes the mandatory sessions with the shrinks.

At around noon we ordered out for some subs and started looking at recent tips and fielding calls. All the other detectives were out scouring the hotels and transport hubs for Richard Kotler. A few silver Mercedes had been pulled over, but they only turned up a doctor from Wilmette, a financial advisor from River Forest and a contractor from Marquette Park. No other messages from that morning. My meatball sub was pretty good, so at least I had that going for me.

At 1:20 Elaina fielded a call that made her sit straight up, put her hand over the receiver and tell me to get on the line. A security guard at the Willis Tower was talking so fast we could hardly understand him. Elaina got him to calm down enough to become intelligible.

He said that there was a guy on the sky deck waving a gun and saying he wanted to kill himself and jump through the glass. The worst of it was that he had a group of high school kids and a couple of teachers held hostage. He said that he was the escort killer and he kind of looked like the guy that we had been searching for.

Elaina asked him if he was being held hostage and he said no, he was in a control room.

She told him to meet us down in the lobby, we would be right there. We literally ran out the door to our assigned car and hit the lights. The patrol dispatcher was alerted, and we pulled up in front of the Willis Tower on South Wacker in about five minutes. There were a couple of patrol cars already there. More were on the way to secure the street and building. We ran into the front entrance and were flagged down by a security officer named Stuart Concerto. He got us into an express elevator to the 103rd floor 1,353 feet above the street. We soon stepped out into a waiting area/gift shop with panoramic views of the city. On a clear day you can see 450 miles in every direction, but we were only looking for the guy with a gun. Anyway, it had been raining most of the day and it was totally overcast.

In an instant we spotted him. He had positioned himself between the school group and the elevator. Some of the kids were still out onto the 4.3 foot glassed in box that gives the sensation of walking on air outside of the tower. I have seen people get excited, even giddy about the experience. These kids, however, were terrified. The man who was somewhere around 50 years old and 6 feet tall with dark hair, wore a long gray overcoat and held a gun to the head of one of the female teachers.

It was at that moment that I realized that I didn't have my gun. It had been collected by the detectives that interviewed me right after the shooting.

Well, Elaina had one if needed, I thought. I wasn't sure whether this guy was Richard Kotler, but I figured we can sort that out later. He spotted us moving in different directions to get him cornered in a small section of the room.

"Stop right there!" he barked.

We slowed down but kept edging a little bit nearer to him. The kids were starting to freak out. Elaina started talking softly to the students nearest to her.

The gunman began raving about someone that drove him to do it. Apparently, she made him do it.

He said, "I had no choice, it was all her fault. It was always their fault, women are evil, they don't care about us. She doesn't care about me. She left me for no good reason so I had to do it."

There was a pause. Some of his hostages began crying quietly. I knew I needed to do something. I held my hands out so that he could see they were empty.

"I know exactly how you feel. Mine left me too," I said loudly, "she is an evil bitch. All I did was love her, and this is what she does to me. She broke my heart. She doesn't care."

I saw him looking at me nodding in agreement.

Elaina was edging ever closer to him. She was creeping like a leopard, sneaking up on a deer.

I put my hands on my head and started whimpering, "I don't think I can take it anymore."

I fell to my knees and some of the students gasped. I looked up at him pitifully, held my arms out and pleaded, "Please just kill me. I can't take it anymore."

He moved his gun from the teachers, headed toward me and Elaina pounced. She grabbed his gun in her left hand, forcing it up toward the ceiling and cracked him over the head with the gun in her right hand. He slumped and let go of his gun. I was up on my feet and caught him before he went down face first. The teacher moved away, seemingly in shock and the students gasped and then cheered. In an instant, Elaina had him cuffed.

In a haze, he started coming around. I picked up the gun he had dropped and looked into his bleary eyes and said, "Man, you really are a dope. No wonder she left you."

He looked incredulously at me and Elaina laughed. "Good, Jack, you had me believing it for a second."

We found a wallet and looked through it before some uniforms took him away. If there was any doubt, we learned that he was not Richard Kotler.

His name was Fred Lamey from Cedar Rapids, Iowa. He had a couple of pictures in his wallet. One of a middle-aged woman, and one of a couple of teenage kids.

I was surprised not to see a prescription for some kind of psychotropic medication. That would all come out in the wash later, I guessed.

We left the rest to the uniformed officers and got onto the express elevator to a standing ovation. I couldn't help thinking sometimes this job really is a fucking rush.

Once off of the elevator, Elaina looked sternly at me. "That was quite a performance, Jack. Where the hell did you come up with that?"

"I've been working on that for years," I said.

She broke down and smiled. "Really, Jack, what were you thinking?"

"Well, first of all, I didn't have much time to think about it. Secondly, I was pretty sure he wasn't our killer or any kind of killer. I didn't think that he really wanted to hurt anyone, just wanted some attention. Someone to listen to him, so I gave that to him. I figured that if I could distract him for just a few seconds, you would jump him. Great job by the way."

She didn't seem convinced. "If he had spotted me, he would've shot us both."

"Yeah," I said, "but I figured there was a better chance that he would shoot the hostage by accident than there was of you screwing it up." She gave herself another sign of the cross.

The elevator door opened on the ground floor and we exited without another word about it.

On the way to our car my phone buzzed, and it was my Uncle Don. He was at his job as the doormen at the Intercontinental Hotel on Michigan Avenue, one of the many places we suspected Richard Kotler may have frequented.

My uncle is a man not easily excited. He had been a 20-year Marine combat Veteran and had pretty much seen it all on the streets of Chicago.

His voice was filled with urgency. "Jackie, you have to get your butt over here now. I mean right now!" he fairly yelled. "He's here."

"Who's here?"

My uncle said, "Your guy, that Kotler character. He just walked into the hotel right past me with a real stunner, a tall brunette."

"Thanks, Uncle Don," I said, "don't try to do anything, keep a lid on this. We'll be right there."

I told Elaina the gist of it and we jumped into the car. Elaina again hit the lights and sound and we sped through the traffic as fast as we safely could. Elaina is a skilled driver. So it wasn't long before we pulled up in front of this classic 1920s luxury hotel.

On the way I remembered the times Uncle Don took me and my brother and sister there at Christmastime to see the magnificent tree and toy-land decorations that were a wonder to my young eyes and mind and how we were able to use the historic old-time swimming pool. It was like walking into a fantasy world from a long-gone era. But this was real, and this was now. Uncle Don opened the side door for us and waved us in.

We ran up to the front desk and asked in unison, "Which room is Richard Kotler's?"

The startled young man immediately went to the keyboard and started typing. He looked up quizzically. "I'm sorry but we don't have a Richard Kotler staying with us."

"That's impossible," I explained, "he just walked in here, a dark-haired, fiftyish guy about six feet tall with a brunette."

He went at it again. "Sorry, sir, there's no one by that name in our system."

A well-dressed short wiry guy in his 40s walked up to us. "I'm Dennis Portman, the Manager, can I help you?"

I explained the situation, he seemed to understand the urgency.

"I can't say that I saw anybody fitting that description. I was up on the 33rd floor of the Executive Tower checking on a complaint about two men shouting at each other in room 3300 but when I got up there, I didn't hear anything. I knocked on the door and the man said that everything was fine. He said they were just arguing over where to go to dinner. The man sounded calm, I let it go."

"What room?" I asked.

"3300," Portman said.

"Can you take me up there?" It wasn't really a question.

"Sure, no problem."

"Elaina, I'll check that out with Portman, you cover everything down here and any common areas."

The Manager, Portman and I hurried from the lobby down the hallway to the right, past Michael Jordan Steakhouse and to the elevators for the Executive Tower. One opened up and a lady with an oversized designer handbag walked out narrowly avoiding us.

As we rushed in Portman tapped the security portal with his card and hit 33. We hurtled up. I called for backup before we reached our floor, and the door opened. An elderly couple and a woman wearing a terrycloth robe and large towel wrapped around her head dressed for the fitness center were waiting to get on and stepped aside as we bounded by zigzagging down the hallway toward room 3300.

Portman knocked hard on the door. He knocked again harder. "This is the Manager, please answer the door." He looked at me and I nodded toward the door. He tapped his card, the green light appeared, and he slowly opened the door. We stepped into a short hallway and walked a few steps and turned right into the spacious bedroom.

I saw a King bed, small couch, a large TV, and windows looking west and south. I could see the Wrigley Building and the Chicago River outside but no one in the room.

The bathroom door off the hallway was closed. I waved Portman back away from me and I gingerly opened the bathroom door, now missing my Beretta for the second time in less than an hour. With very little pressure applied, the door swung open much quicker than I'd intended. I tensed for an unknown confrontation. Nothing to be seen other than a bathtub, a walk-in shower, the toilet and another large window.

What the hell, I thought as I came out of the bathroom and started turning left back into the bedroom. I found myself face-to-face with the large double door of the hallway closet. I pulled one of the two shiny silver cylindrical door handles attached to one of the twin gray slatted closet doors. As soon as I opened the door on the right side. I immediately threw open the door on the left, and there he was.

Richard Kotler's eyes were bugging out of his head, his face and lips were blue, and his tongue was simply sticking out of his mouth. He was being hung up with a man's tie around his neck which was wrapped around the closet pole. His bare feet were touching the closet floor and he was wearing only some black boxer shorts.

I called for Portman, directing him to lift Kotler up as much as he could while I untied the makeshift noose around his neck. We laid Kotler down on the carpet and I checked for a pulse, but he was gone. I then realized that I had recognized the woman wearing the terrycloth robe.

"Portman, give me your pass card," I ordered. He hesitated, but the look I gave him made it clear to him. He handed it over.

"Call 911 and ask for an ambulance."

"But he is dead," he said.

"Just do it."

I bolted for the elevators and hit the down button. The 18 seconds it took for an elevator to appear seemed like an hour. When it finally showed up, everything seemed to be moving in slow motion. How fucking long does it take for an elevator door to open? I tapped the card, hit FC, and the door seemed to close inch by inch. The elevator started descending. I counted the floors 32,31, 30,29 then it stopped at 28 I can't believe this. Two goofing looking teenage boys laughing without a care in the world got on. One of the boys hit L then the lazy door closed again, 27,26, 25 24, then it stopped at 23. My fucking God no! A young woman with a roller suitcase entered and I hit the close door button and she looked at me like I was crazy which by then I was. At long last the elevator stopped at the fitness center and everyone pressed themselves into the sides of the elevator to let the crazy man out.

I looked right and then left, saw the glass doors to the fitness center and ran up to them and began pulling on the long vertical grips. They were locked! I realized that I needed to tap in, so I went to the security mechanism on the wall, tapped it with Portman's card and then the fitness center door magically opened. *What an idiot,* I thought, I hadn't been there in years so I wasn't sure where to look. I ran down a flight of stairs into the locker rooms. I went by the unmanned desk and found myself with the choice of men's or women's locker rooms. I went with the men's. I ran in, looked in a sauna room and three showers then the locker room area. Nothing but a 70-year-old guy fighting with his socks. I ran back out into the hall. The hell with it, I ran into the women's locker room expecting to be verbally and possibly physically assaulted, but to my relief there was no one in there. I did take a few harsh words from a couple of short middle-aged women coming in as I exited but there was no time for explanations.

I recalled having to go up to the pool, so I ran up the first set of stairs that I saw which connected at a right angle to another flight going up. At that level I could hear the whizzing of the exercise room and walked in to see a couple of young guys running treadmills and a young blonde woman lifting weights I moved up the stairs and saw an opening and it came back to me that this was the way to the pool. I leapt up the short set of steps and came out into the amazing pool setting of the Intercontinental Hotel. I heard a woman's voice to my right yelling, "She's killing her, help!"

I looked to my left and then what I saw and heard was blood curdling. It was Valentina in the shallow end of the pool. She was wearing a white t-shirt and underpants with her back to me. I heard a loud, deep angry male voice shout, "Die, you pretty pitch, I'll kill you!" I ran toward her and I could see that she was holding a woman by the throat and under the water the woman was flailing and struggling and then went limp. My God, it was Elaina! I ran toward the pool throwing off my coat when I got about four feet from Valentina, I took a flying dive onto her knocking her off of my partner. I dragged Elaina to the side of the pool and used all of my energy to lift her up over the foot and a half wall above the waterline. In all of her wet clothes she was amazingly heavy. I got her onto the pool deck but before I could get out to attend to her, I felt a viselike grip being applied to my throat by Valentina's right arm. I heard a deep gravelly angry voice swearing and promising to break my neck and kill me. That was the last thing I heard before being pulled under the water. My body was fully in the water about a foot under. I was trying to twist myself free, but her grip was too strong. The situation was dire, but I knew I couldn't panic. I was in the shallow end, and somehow, I had to get my feet to the bottom to propel myself up above the water line to get some air. I pulled my legs into my chest and arched my back as hard as I could, then pushing my feet down and extending my legs I reached just enough of the pool bottom to thrust my body up and out of the water enough to breathe and reach my left hand behind my head. I frantically reached to find her face. I first felt her chin then worked my hand further up her face and then as hard as I could I put two fingers into her eyes. She roared like a wounded lion her grip loosened and I broke free she roared again and lunged toward me like an enraged animal. Her face met the strongest straight right-hand punch I could muster. It landed just above her nose right between her eyes she went limp, knocked out cold.

Now I had to drag her to the side of the pool and get her out of the water. Fortunately, she wasn't as fully clothed as Elaina and I was able to slide her out of the pool and onto the deck only a few feet away from my motionless partner. There was no time to lose. I pulled myself out and immediately started performing CPR on Elaina. I saw no movement in her chest and started to apply hand compressions. After about a minute I pinched her nose with my left hand and made sure her mouth was cleared with my right. I placed my mouth securely over hers and blew hard twice I noticed two uniformed officers emerge from the stairway onto the deck and yelled for them to call for another bus and to check on her pointing to Valentina and to place her under arrest I began more compressions on Elaina and started pleading with her to, "Cough, cough! Breathe, breathe!" then, finally, after another couple of mouth-to-mouth blows and more compressions got her coughing and water spurted out of her mouth and nose. I screamed yeah! I turned her on her side and patted her back. She stopped convulsing and coughing and just started spitting and laboring to breathe. At that moment Valentina started coming around and I yelled at the uniforms to get her up and cuffed. Elaina stopped spitting and began breathing normally. She struggled to sit up and she was blinking and looking around as if trying to figure out what in the hell happened. After a minute she seemed to clear her head and realize where she was. "My God, Jack, I'm so sorry, she was so quick Before I knew it, she had control of me and dragged me into the water with her. I have never seen a woman with such strength, not many men either. Jack, you saved my life."

"Hey, now we're even, partner. Besides, we got her, we got the escort killer; we did it!"

She said, "Hell yeah, right there." I pointed to Valentina, who was now sitting up, coughing, rocking herself back and forth and sobbing.

"Her, yeah her. She left Kotler up in room 3300 hung up by one of his neckties in the closet. When she was holding you under, she was growling and sounding like a deep voiced man. Now look at her, she seems like a frightened little girl."

Elaina got to her feet and said, "Diablo."

"Maybe so," I said, "she's definitely certifiable."

More uniforms and EMTs started pouring in. Elaina didn't want to, but I insisted that she go to the hospital and get checked out. I told her that I would see her later at the station. She agreed reluctantly and went with the EMTs.

Another pair of EMTs were tending to Valentina who didn't respond coherently to any of their questions. I told them to get her checked out immediately and then get her a psychiatric eval at Northwestern Memorial under heavy security. I added, "Make sure she is considered extremely dangerous." They placed Valentina on a gurney and wheeled her down the stairs and out to the elevator with the help of one of the officers.

By the time they all left I realized manager Dennis Portman and I were the only ones left. I thanked him for his help and asked him to give me a few minutes alone. He said certainly and disappeared down the stairs. I noticed my jacket on the deck and picked it up. It was the only somewhat dry article of clothing that I had. I walked up a few steps and sat down in the first row of the three-deck viewing area built I suppose in the 20s for gentlemen's swimming competitions. I rummaged through the pocket of my damp jacket and was happy to find my phone in working order. I made the call to the station, and Sgt. Clyde Simpson answered right away. "Jack, I heard you are okay."

"I'm fine, Sarge, we got the son of a bitch it turned out to be a woman, another escort. She's under wraps. You should be able to find her at Northwestern Memorial getting a psychiatric eval. She's batshit crazy, some kind of split personality, I guess. I don't know. I'm sure that the shrinks will have a lot to say. I just need a few minutes to decompress. I'll be at the station in a little while to write my report."

"No problem, Jack, take your time. Great work."

"Thanks, Sarge. Elaina was roughed up pretty good, almost drowned, but she is okay. I made her go with the EMTs to get checked out; you'll probably see her soon."

"Okay, Jack. Again, great job!"

I sat back and breathed a big sigh of relief. *Holy crap, look at this place,* I thought, what a wild atmosphere: Art Deco meets ancient classical Greek columns, Roman arches, and fake fountains. Everything in imitation white marble. And on the other side of the pool a seven-foot ribbon of 1920s colorful tile and two card tables with imitation wicker chairs and Art Deco light fixtures. I let my mind wander. I imagined the Roman Emperor Nero sitting at one of the card tables playing a game of dice with Al Capone for all the marbles. Two of the most ruthless characters of all time. For a moment I wondered who would win. But it was no contest. My money was on the Chicago guy.

Chapter 13

I came out of a deep sleep Saturday morning at 8:00 in a hazy state of mind. My phone was buzzing, but I didn't want to answer. I hadn't slept soundly in over a week and I just didn't want to let it go. The phone kept buzzing and after a few determined minutes of ignoring it, I gave in.

"Hello," I said sounding righteously perturbed, "oh, hi, Dad. Yeah, I'm fine."

"How is your partner?" he asked. "They said on the news that she almost drowned."

"Well, she did," I answered, "but she's okay now. She got checked out at the hospital and I saw her again later at the station before we sent her home. Of course. that meant I had to do the reports on Willis Tower and the Intercontinental," I said with a laugh.

"You had quite a week for yourself, Jackie, you have had us worried sick. Molly and Barry too."

"I know, Dad, never a dull moment, right?"

"I hope you can keep it a little less interesting for a while."

"Don't worry, I'll try. It's the job, Dad. Anyway, Lieutenant Whitehead gave us the whole weekend off. The whole task force too."

"Call Molly, will you?" he asked. "She's a wreck."

"Okay, Dad, will do."

I started looking at texts and emails and it was overwhelming; these would have to wait. I checked my voicemail and listened to a few messages including one from my sister Molly.

Then I heard Morgan Latner's voice. "Hey, man, are you ready for our game this morning? It's the championship buddy! I'll pick you up at ten."

Crap, I had completely forgotten about the basketball game, our league championship no less. Oh boy, my motivation on a scale of 1 to 10 was about a zero. I was exhausted and distracted but I had to rally. I am the captain of the team, one of the best players.

"Okay, Fallon, get going."

I looked out the window for the first time that morning and saw sunny skies for a change. I jumped in the shower and finished it with a cold soak. I was snapping out of it, focusing. I ate some cereal and felt pretty good. I got Latner on the phone and accepted his offer of a ride to the game. Ricky Del Signore was next and he sounded excited. I left a message for Molly and sat down in my living room with some easy listening music, Nora Jones, put me into a relaxed mood and I felt content for the first time in what seemed like a very, very, long time. I nodded off and was startled when my phone buzzed again and it was Morgan Latner asking me to come down. I grabbed my gym bag, gave a quick check for my team shirt and shoes and quickly left my apartment.

Downstairs the doorman greeted me as he usually does, then added, "Nice going, Jack," I said, "Thanks," and walked out to see Latner waiting right in front.

I got in, we bumped fists and said, "Let's do it."

We rode to the Rogers Park Gym without saying much, listening to Latner's hip hop. When we got there, all of the team members were either already there or arriving when we did. I thought that was a good sign. Some of the guys came dressed to play and others like Latner and myself got dressed there. We all went into the locker room together.

Our opponents all seemed to be there and dressed to play. They stayed together on the other side of the small bleachers section.

Inside the locker room everyone was pretty quiet. A couple of guys came up to me and shook hands or offered a high five without a word said. There was no talk about the job, we were all about the game.

I called out the usual starting five and our usual man-to-man defense. We decided to press them full court after they made free throws but otherwise we were going to use a straight half-court man-to-man. We had seen enough of our opponents to know that they were more athletic but less physical than the team we had just played in the semi's.

We matched up pretty well with them in height, but they were going to be a little quicker and faster. At least they didn't have anyone as good as Jackie Gilchrist.

Despite how locked in we all were, we started out sluggishly. None of us were hitting from the outside but we were able to score on some drives and inside shots. They were rebounding from a missed shot well and fast, breaking early for some easy baskets.

Our full court press didn't work either, so we pulled that early. At the end of the first half, we were down by 10. They went over to the bleachers congratulating each other and we went into the locker room in a foul mood. Everyone was pissed off but under control. We were a pretty close-knit team and all the guys were used to tough situations.

After waiting a couple of minutes to let the guys calm down a little, I stood up and said, "Okay, we know we can play much better than this. We need to control the boards so they will not be able to run that fast break on us. Morgan and Nick. that's going to be mostly on you because we are going switch to three guards, Anton is going to be the third guard with me and Ricky. Here's the plan on defense. We are going to make a point of calling out our man every time as they come down with the ball. We are going to make it look like we are playing our usual half-court man-to-man, but as soon as the ball crosses the half-court line, whoever is next to the ball will force his man to one side.

Then the closest other guard will jump the ball for a double-team. The weak side guard will have to decide to cover the crosscourt pass to their other guard or get in front of their high post. Morgan will have to play a centerfield to take away a pass, mainly to the wings and Perkins will have to cut off anything easy to the basket. Of course, we all will need to shoot better. Last thing is, we all know at least one or all of the great cops we lost in the last couple of days. Let's put our hands in for Skinner Dolan and Wilkes."

We all put our hands together and yelled their names, finishing with "Let's go!" We started the second half on fire. Latner and I hit our first few shots and the half-court press, surprised them for a while, allowing us to get a couple of steals and easy baskets. Five minutes into the second half we tied the game.

They figured out the press and we had to call it off, but by that time we had momentum and we didn't give it up. Morgan and Perkins controlled the boards and our defense was stifling.

They recovered their poise eventually, but it was too late. We kept hitting our shots and even Ricky and Anton, who normally didn't shoot much, hit a couple of shots. We got the lead and never gave it up, winning by eight points. The horn sounded and there were high-fives and some hugs all around. We shook hands with our opponents and joyously went back to the locker room. Everyone agreed to meet at Timothy O'Toole's at two. Some of us hit the showers and the other guys went home to do the same. Morgan dropped me off at home and offered to pick me up an hour later, Normally I wanted to drive myself, but I knew that he didn't drink much and after the week I'd just had, I knew that I would.

"Okay. buddy, see you in an hour." I grabbed our team trophy that the League Manager handed me on the way out of the gym with the promise to have our champions jackets ready in a couple of weeks. An hour later I was back down in front of my building with the trophy getting back into Latner's car.

I lifted the trophy and said, "I guess this really belongs at O'Toole's."

We drove downtown in a much lighter mood than we had driving to the game.

Morgan wanted to know how everything went down on Friday and got a laugh out of the incident at Willis Tower. We got a parking spot on Fairbanks and walked into O'Toole's, down the stairs and into the large main barroom. The place was packed. Morgan and I looked at each other with the what the hell look.

I knew right away that this was not about our basketball team but instinctively I raised the trophy up over my head anyway, causing a raucous cheer.

My brother Barry walked up to us and said, "Way to go, guys. I thought the Near North needed a little diversion, so I put this together last night. Nice that the team came through."

I handed him the trophy and said, "Here, find a place for this."

Morgan and I waded into the crowd and went our separate ways. The whole place was full of cops from the Near North and elsewhere. I was greeted with congratulations by a dozen friends and acquaintances before I got to John Youngblood.

He was seated at the bar and stood up, my level of emotion rose with him and we hugged for a long moment and I could see the hurt in his eyes.

"I am so sorry about, Larry," I said, "you guys saved my life."

He looked pained. "You're not supposed to lose your partner, man. I tried so hard to put some sense into him, but he was so headstrong. You know more balls than brains." He patted me on the back. "Glad to hear that you didn't lose Rodriguez, thank God for that, Jack."

"Well, she saved my ass the first day," I said, "it's hard to believe she only came to the Near North a couple of weeks ago, so much has gone down."

Elaina waved to me. "There she is now. John, thanks again, I am grateful."

He sat down and I made my way through the crowd to where Elaina was at a table with Zileen and Henrique. There was a seat and I sat down. We had a group high five and I took one of the available glasses and poured a beer from one of the pitchers on the table. Our usual free pitchers after a win were irrelevant since O'Toole's was giving us an open bar from two to four.

I raised my glass and said, "To the Task Force. We got our man or in this case, our woman."

We clinked glasses and I took a long drink. It really tasted great.

"How did you know it was her, Jack, what tipped you off?" Zileen asked. "Honestly, I didn't know until we found Richard Kotler hung up with his own necktie in the closet of his room.

"Then it hit me like a ton of bricks. Coming out of the elevator on the 33rd floor, a woman in a bathrobe and towel wrapped around her head was waiting to get on. She looked vaguely familiar, but it didn't dawn on me until we saw Kotler and I realized it couldn't have been him. We had interviewed the escort Valentina Brunner after the murder at Ohio Street Beach and the image of her face flashed before my eyes. I was pretty sure that she was headed to the pool and fitness center, so I rushed down there. I was worried that she might go after somebody else but had not thought it could be Elaina, I just found them in the nick of time."

"She completely overpowered me," Elaina said. "My partner here saved me."

"She almost got me too," I said with a laugh, "it took everything I had to get her off me."

Henrique chimed in, "You are a hero, Detective Fallon. When I become mayor, you will be in charge of my security."

He was serious but the three of us laughed anyway. "I'll take that as a compliment, Henrique."

I saw my dad across the crowded room and excused myself. I wrestled my way through the crowd that continued to grow and gave him a hug. It was that kind of day. He told me how glad he was to see me in one piece and I told him how happy I was that he was there.

I asked them if Molly was coming and was informed that she was away for the weekend at a conference in Boston for Northwestern. She had gotten my message and was as relieved as he was. I saw Sergeant Simpson waving at me and told Dad I would check in with him later.

I made it to where Clyde Simpson was sitting at a booth. He invited me to join them, he poured me a beer and we took a drink.

"I want you to know that the brass are very happy about how the task force handled this case, Jack. They want you and Elaina at their press conference Monday. You both are receiving some commendations. I think the whole task force will be receiving something but they want you and Rodriguez to be the face of it. I want you to know that I think it is well deserved. We all do."

"Thanks, Sergeant."

I stood up and said that I wanted to try to say hello to some old friends and he waved me off and I turned around and was face-to-face with an old enemy instead.

"Hey," I blurted out starting to move around him.

"Hold on a minute," Koz said gruffly. "I want to talk to you."

Oh boy, I thought, *not today.* "You know I never liked you, Fallon."

"Yeah, I know," I replied.

Then he continued. "But after I seen what you done this past couple of days, I've gotta say something, kid. You're okay." He held out his hand and I shook it.

"I really appreciate that," I said. Strangely. I really meant it.

Just then there was a stirring in the crowd and people started looking toward the entrance. The bar music fell silent and then the faint sounds of bagpiping could be heard over the din of the crowd. Then it grew louder. Two pipers walked through the entrance and somehow the throng parted. They were in the middle of the room and the sweet sounds of 'Oh Danny Boy' came in and swirled throughout O'Toole's.

Every nook and cranny and heart was filled with its sweet melancholy. The bartenders and servers had planned their attack flawlessly and soon everyone had a shot of Jameson in their hand. The pipers gently finished their song. Brother Barry took over. "Thank you all for being here today in celebration of what Chicago's finest do every day, but especially to those we have lost just the last two days. Let's raise our glasses to say thank you and goodbye to Larry Skinner, Ryan Dolan, and Naomi Wilkes."

"Hear, hear!" Everyone drank and cheered and the piping went on and it was an emotional and joyous Irish wake of a day.

Around 8:30 I found myself being driven home on Lakeshore Drive. It was a clear cold night outside and a warm hazy night inside the car and my mind. Once back at my building on North Clarendon, Morgan Latner and I exchanged one last high five and I started walking into my building. Something told me to turn back around and I walked up Clarendon to Lawrence and turned left; even in my fog I knew where I was going. I crossed the street at Broadway and headed for the funky neon lights of the Green Mill. I sauntered into the iconic bar to the sounds of jazz and the vision of Emma sitting at the end of the bar. As if by something preordained, a guy sitting next to her got up, took his drink off the bar and went to sit at a nearby table. I didn't hesitate to go directly to her and sit down. I couldn't get myself to say anything to her. Even in my emotional and alcoholic state, she made me nervous and I didn't get nervous. Finally, she had mercy on me. "What's happening, detective?" she said laughing.

"Not much," I managed to get out of my mouth.

She laughed again. "Come on, Detective Jack Fallon, I don't even watch the news and you have been everywhere. It's been impossible not to hear about what you have been up to."

Now I laughed. "I thought you were asking about my love life," I quipped, and this time we both laughed.

"Well, you know so much about me but I don't know anything about you," I said.

"What do you want to know?" she said.

"Well, what is your last name."

"It's Merlin," she told me.

"Emma Merlin," I marveled, "That's very magical," I said clumsily and immediately regretted it.

"Very clever, Jack."

I smiled. "I know, I know, that's me all right; I guess you never heard that before?"

Luckily, Gus Kezios came over to break that train of thought. "What will you have?" he asked.

"I'll have a Miller and whatever Emma would like," I told him. He brought me my beer and some kind of a martini for Emma. After that everything became natural and easy, the drinks and conversation flowed and time flew by. I learned that she was an artist and an actress, she can make sculptures out of clay plaster or steel. She could sing, do stand-up comedy and who knew what else. I had never met such a free spirit. I hardly even noticed how beautiful she was. For a while everything seemed right. I don't know what the hell she learned about me. I was just glad she stayed.

Before I knew it, Gus was cleaning and wiping the bar, making last call. I paid the tab and we got up to leave. As we did, Gus said, "Take care of yourself, Detective. See you next time, Emma," he called out as we walked out into the clear, cold Chicago night.

We just started walking east on Lawrence, and after a couple of blocks she stopped. "Can I walk you home?" I practically pleaded.

She looked at me warmly but firmly and said, "No. This is where the story ends for tonight, Jack Fallon." She turned and walked across Lawrence and down a dimly lit side street fading into the night. She left me standing on a corner in Uptown at 3:00 a.m. All I could think of was this may be good night, Emma Merlin, but it is not goodbye.

Epilogue

On the following Saturday one of the largest ceremonies ever held in Chicago for fallen police officers was held downtown. As it so happened all three of the officers were Catholic and the Archdiocese reached out to the families who all agreed to a joint funeral to be held at Holy Name Cathedral with a procession down Wabash and then veering over to Grant Park. Earlier in the week all of the detectives from the task force were given police medals and Elaina and I were also given awards of valor for our work bringing down the mugging gang.

Sophie called a couple of times leaving messages asking to see me. As tempting as it was, I knew it wasn't a good idea. Hell, it wasn't a good idea the first time. She had been right about Valentina's mother, though. She was diagnosed with schizophrenia when Valentina was a teenager, causing her to be institutionalized in Austria. Valentina was hit hard by her mother's absence and turned all of her energy into bodybuilding and weight training. She had engaged in weightlifting and bodybuilding competitions throughout Europe and was very successful until her coach was accused of providing athletes with steroids and other performance-enhancing drugs and he was forced to retire from the sport. Valentina stopped competitive bodybuilding shortly thereafter and was soon working as a personal trainer to celebrities and powerful business people in Austria and Germany before coming to the U.S. to work at one of Chicago's most prestigious health clubs. Since then she had developed an impressive list of clients as a personal trainer.

She has now been diagnosed with dissociative identity disorder, also known as DID and more commonly as multiple personality disorder. She is being held at the in-patient psychiatric center at the University of Illinois Department of Psychiatry's secure facility. Richard Kotler had never harmed anyone except of course the company he helped to manage. He embezzled $12 million and had it transferred it to Brazil but got caught up in the escort murders before he could transfer himself out of the U.S. He had stolen one of his partner's IDs and credit cards but was stuck in Chicago waiting to get himself a phony passport. In the meantime, he couldn't control his addiction to escorts which eventually got him killed.

Elaina and I have been moved to the homicide unit permanently, which is fine with us. It is good to have a strong partner and of course we are both thrilled to know that we will be able to work with Koz from time to time. I haven't seen Emma Merlin again but she left an invitation to an art exhibit showing her sculptures and paintings with Gus at the Green Mill. It will be held in June at a Gold Coast art gallery. I have never been to an art showing before but somehow, I think I will be attending this one.